I0640505

LAWFULLY JUSTIFIED

A BOUNTY HUNTER LAWKEEPER ROMANCE

LORANA HOOPES

THE
LAWKEEPERS

This book is dedicated to all the hardworking law enforcement officers out there. Our world would not be as safe without all of you.

And to my family who lets me sacrifice time with them to write these stories in my head.

Thank you so much for picking up this book. I hope you enjoy the story and the characters as they are dear to my heart. If you do, please leave a review at your retailer. It really does make a difference because it lets people make an informed decision about books. Below are the other books in this series. I would love for you to check them out. I'd also like to offer you a sample of my newest book. Free Sample!

Lawkeepers series:

Lawfully Matched

The Scarlet Wedding

Lawfully Redeemed

Lawfully Pursued

CHAPTER ONE

William "Wild Bill" Cook smoothed his black duster and stepped through the swinging batwing doors into the saloon. His eyes scanned the bustling, noisy room for the slim, bearded man whose face he had memorized from the Wanted Poster, but he didn't appear to be in the room. Of course, that meant nothing. Sometimes the men tried to disguise themselves or hide in low lit corners. Occasionally, he even found them upstairs with one of the saloon girls, if they had the money. Once he had even found a mark upstairs pretending to be a saloon girl. He hadn't been the brightest one, not realizing his full beard was a dead giveaway. It didn't matter. Wild Bill Cook always got his man.

He sidled up to the bar, pulled his black hat low on his eyes, and ordered a Whiskey. He wasn't a big drinker - his wife had hated the stuff - but he found one drink honed his senses and allowed him to survey the room without standing out too much. The last thing he needed was someone recognizing he didn't belong and warning Frank Monroe. The man was a cattle thief, and no man liked the prospect of jail time and most fought tooth and nail not to go.

When the drink slid his way, William picked it up, trying to ignore the cloudy film on it - Catherine would roll over in her grave if she saw him drinking from such a cup - and adjusted his position so that his back was to the bar.

A heated poker game was taking place at a table across the room, but a closer look ruled out any of those men. Another few men sat at a table closer to his position, tossing back beers, but they were all too large to be his mark. His eyes continued to scan left, but after coming up empty, he finished his drink and turned back to the bartender. Monroe must be hiding out upstairs then.

"Who do you have working tonight?" William asked the bartender. "It's been a long ride, and I'd like to unwind."

The long-haired bartender smiled at him,

revealing a bottom row of crooked teeth. "What's your flavor?"

William shook his head as he spun the glass on the counter. "I'm not particular. What are my choices?"

The bartender scanned the room. "Looks like we have two blonds, Nellie and Lizzie, down here which means Minnie, my brunette is upstairs, engaged in other business."

"I guess I'll take a blond then," William said.

"Nellie," the bartender hollered across the noisy room. He cocked his head in a "come here" gesture, and a moment later, a plump blond appeared at William's side.

Her blond hair was pinned to one side and curled. Bright red lipstick covered her lips along with a dark rouge. A blood red dress trimmed in a black fringe hugged her frame a little too tightly, sending her extra flesh rolling over the top. William forced his eyes to remain on her face.

"You looking for a good time, honey?" she asked, laying a hand on his arm.

William resisted the urge to shake her hand off. She was his ticket upstairs, and he could swallow his revulsion a moment longer to apprehend his man.

"Sure am. Are you good at giving one?"

"I'm good at everything, honey." Her voice flowed like silk out of her mouth, but it had no effect on William. He hadn't been with a woman since the death of his wife, and he wouldn't until he married again. IF he married again.

"Lead the way then," he said, pushing the glass back to the bartender and standing. Nellie headed for the back stairs, sashaying her ample hips as she walked. William kept his eyes peeled for Monroe as he followed her, just in case he had missed the man in his initial scan. It didn't happen often, but William stayed alive by always checking twice if the opportunity presented itself.

With each step, the wooden stairs groaned under his weight and William held tight to the railing as he climbed. The top of the stairs opened into a small hallway. Two doors were on the left and two were on the right, but all were closed. How was he going to determine which room Monroe was in?

"Do you girls all have a regular room?" William asked, hoping her answer would let him know which room Monroe was in.

"Sort of," Nellie said with a shrug, "but there are three other girls, so we have to share."

Not helpful. He'd have to be more direct. "Which

one is Minnie's regular room?" William narrowed his eyes as he listened, but he heard no sound coming from any of the rooms.

Nellie's smile faded, and she crossed her arms. "Are you here for Minnie or for me?"

William scanned her face. While he didn't trust her - he trusted no one - he had little choice but to ask for her help if he wanted any chance of surprising Monroe. "Honestly ma'am, I'm here for the man who is with Minnie. If you can point out her room, I'll pay you for your time."

Nellie's eyes widened and then she smiled. "Sure, her room is the second one on the left."

William tipped his hat and headed that direction. His right hand fell to the hilt of his revolver as his left turned the handle. Monroe and a brunette turned his direction as the door opened.

"Run, Frank," Nellie shouted from behind William.

A look of surprise followed by a flash of fear crossed Monroe's face before he rolled out of the bed and dove for cover. With a grumble, William whipped his gun out. He hated when things didn't go according to plan. "Frank Monroe, you're coming with me. You're wanted for stealing cattle."

The brunette pulled the sheet around her and let out a blood-curdling scream. The noise distracted William just enough that he didn't see Nellie run up behind him until it was too late. She rammed him with her shoulder, sending him into the door jamb.

A shot went off, followed by two more female screams. William thought at first that he had fired his gun when Nellie hit him, but then the searing pain just above his clavicle hit him. Monroe sat on the floor, his gun smoking in his hand. William tried to raise his arm to fire a shot, but it would no longer obey his command.

As soon as Monroe realized he had the upper hand, he scrambled up, but before he could make it very far, the thunder of footsteps reached the second floor.

"What's going on here?" the bartender demanded, splotches of red lighting up his face and emphasizing the scar that resided there.

"That's Frank Monroe," William said, gritting his teeth through the pain. "He's a wanted man, and I'm bringing him in. This one ought to be under arrest for abetting a felon." He pointed at Nellie with his left hand, trying to ward off the darkness that was creeping in on his vision.

"You can't arrest my girl," the bartender roared.

"Actually, we can," a male voice said from behind the bartender. Before the darkness won the battle, William noticed a star pinned to the man's chest. At least his man wouldn't get away.

CHAPTER TWO

E mma was just finishing wrapping the bandages when the door of the clinic swung open. Deputy Jennings and Sheriff Johnson stepped in, supporting a dark-haired man between them. Blood ran from a hole in the skin above his clavicle.

"Pa," Emma hollered as she pointed to the cot in the front room. Her father thundered in from the back room a moment later. "Who is he?" she asked.

"A bounty hunter. He was trying to apprehend Frank Monroe when he was shot."

"Emma, get me a wet rag," her father said as he crouched in front of the cot. "I can't see the wound through all the blood."

Emma grabbed a clean towel and soaked it in the

wash basin. After giving it a quick wring out, she hurried it over to her father.

He began wiping away the dried blood and cleaning out the wound. The unconscious man moaned but his eyes remained closed. Emma bit her lip as she watched the blood continue to pour out of the hole. She wasn't squeamish about injuries, but she hated watching people die and gunshot wounds were often fatal.

"Can you pick him up?" her father asked. "I need to see if the bullet exited the other side."

The two men did as he asked, and Emma peered over their shoulders. There was an exit wound, slightly larger and spouting even more blood, but it wasn't as large as she expected. She had little experience with gunshot wounds, but she was almost certain not all the bullet had come out the other side.

"Emma, get my glasses and the tweezers please."

Emma hurried over to the desk and grabbed his glasses off the top, then opened the drawer to find the tweezers.

He put the glasses on and peered closer to the wound before taking the tweezers and poking inside the wound. A few metal fragments dropped on to the bed beside the man. Her father made another pass, but this time the metal instrument returned empty.

"I'm afraid there are more fragments," he said, shaking his head sadly, "but I can't see them. The best I can do now is stitch him up and hope for the best."

"And pray," Deputy Jennings added.

Her father nodded and motioned for Emma to grab the needle and thread. She sent up a silent prayer for the unknown man as she did. After splashing a little alcohol on the wound, her father began to stitch first the entrance and then the exit wound. If the man survived, he would have quite the scar. He was lucky the bullet had hit where it did. Any further down and it would have shattered his clavicle. Any to the left and it would have torn open his neck. Somehow the bullet had managed to slice cleanly through only flesh, missing both muscles and bones.

"I'm afraid that's all I can do for him," her father said as he finished. Emma handed him a clean towel to wipe his hands on. "Did you at least catch the fella for him?"

"We did," Sheriff Johnson said with a nod. "We also had to bring in Nellie Watson too as she evidently warned the fugitive and attacked the bounty hunter here. We'll have to find out what that was about."

"Indeed," her father said. "Well, I'll stay with our friend here tonight, and we'll see how his condition is tomorrow. As long as we avoid an infection, he should heal alright, but it's a good thing you brought him in as quickly as you did."

The sheriff and the deputy tipped their hats before exiting the clinic.

"Why don't you head home, Emma? I'm sure the others will be wanting dinner soon."

The others consisted of her younger siblings. Samuel who was twenty, Carrie at sixteen, Benjamin who was twelve, and Jennie brought up the rear at six. It had been Jennie's birth that had taken their mother, and Emma had stepped in to be the mothering role. It was probably one reason why she wanted children of her own so badly.

Carrie was old enough now to be taking on the homestead responsibilities. In fact, she had taken over when Emma married, but after Joseph died and Emma moved back home, Carrie had let Emma take over cooking dinner and putting Jennie to bed again.

"Okay, Pa, let me just soak these towels so the blood doesn't stain." Emma gathered the bloody cloths and dumped them in the wash basin. Hopefully, the soak overnight would remove the blood and she could scrub them in the morning. "Will you be home at all tonight, Pa?"

"No, I'll probably stay with him tonight. I don't

know if he'll make it through the night and no man should die alone. You can take my place tomorrow and I'll get some sleep then."

"Okay, Pa." Emma hugged him and planted a quick kiss on his cheek. "See you in the morning."

The sun was just dropping below the buildings as Emma exited the clinic. Normally she loved the red, orange, and purple that colored the West Texas sky and she spent her time pondering the greatness of God to create such beautiful colors, but tonight her attention was consumed by the unknown man.

Who was he? Did he have a family waiting for him somewhere? She hated the thought of him dying in this town where no one seemed to know who he was. Emma thought back to the night Joseph had told her he was taking a job with the Rangers.

"Why do you have to go?" she asked.

"It's my duty," Joseph said. "When I signed up with the Rangers, it wasn't just to protect the town I live in. It was to be available for service whenever needed. This time, they need my help rounding up a dangerous man. He's robbed and tortured dozens of people. Those people need my help."

Emma bit her lip. She knew his Ranger position was important to him, but they'd only been married a month and now he was leaving. "Do you know how long you might be gone?" she asked in a small voice.

"As long as it takes," he said, planting a kiss on her forehead, "but my best guess is a week, maybe two."

A week. She could handle a week. The day would keep her busy with cleaning and sewing. Maybe she could even help her father out. It was more the nights she worried about. "Okay, be safe, and remember that I love you," she said, pasting what she hoped was a brave smile on her face.

"I love you too."

The week had turned into nearly two and Emma had lain awake each of those nights wondering if he would ever come home. And then her worst nightmare had come true, and the night had come when he never returned home. Was there a woman somewhere right now worrying as Emma had back then?

"Hi, Emma, I hope you don't mind, but I started dinner," Carrie said when Emma entered the house a few minutes later. While one day she hoped to have her own house again, for now, Emma enjoyed living right on the edge of town. It allowed her to walk to her father's clinic without having to bother with a horse.

"Of course I don't mind. You're welcome to make dinner any day you'd like," Emma said, smiling at her younger sister. "You are an amazing cook."

"Well, I'm not as good as you," Carrie said,

blushing and dropping her head, "but you had Ma around a little longer to learn from."

Emma wrapped her arm around the girl, a younger version of herself with long blond hair and green eyes. "I'm sorry you didn't have Ma as long as I did, but you are just as good a cook as I am. Maybe even better."

"Emma!" Jennie's excited voice echoed through the small house, and a moment later, the girl appeared, her dark hair flying behind her. Jennie was the spitting image of their mother with her brown hair and blue eyes. While Emma couldn't fault her for it, seeing Jennie always pulled at Emma's heartstrings and made her miss their mother more.

"Hi Jennie Bean," Emma said, squatting down to hug the girl.

"I'm not a bean," Jennie said laughing. Though this was a nightly game with them, Jennie never seemed to tire of it.

"You're not?" Emma feigned surprise.

"No, I'm a girl." Jennie put her little hands on her hips and turned her nose up in the air.

"Well, be a good girl and go call your brothers in for supper."

Jennie nodded and spun on her heel, hollering as she went. "Benjamin, Samuel, supper's ready."

"Not quite what I had in mind," Emma said with a chuckle and a shake of her head.

"Is Pa not coming for dinner?" Carrie asked as she headed to the kitchen.

"No, there was an altercation at the saloon tonight and a man was shot. Pa is staying to watch him and be there in case he passes in the night."

Carrie's hand flew to her mouth, and her eyes grew large and round. "Oh, how awful."

Emma nodded. "It is, and I keep wondering if he has family out there somewhere wondering where he is."

"Did it remind you of Joseph?" Carrie asked as she pulled dishes from the cupboard.

A sad smile played across Emma's lips. "It did, but then a lot of things remind me of Joseph."

"Do you think you'll ever marry again?" Carrie asked in a soft voice as she dished up the stew.

"Maybe one day," Emma said, taking the full bowls to the table, "if God sends me the right man."

CHAPTER THREE

William smiled at Catherine as they walked through the tall grass. The sun was especially bright today, and he couldn't remember a time she looked more beautiful. Golden threads sparkled in her hair as if the sun had kissed her strands itself. Her hazel eyes twinkled as she smiled at him.

"I thought I'd never see you again," he said as he took her hand, her perfect, porcelain, dainty hand.

"I'm always here watching you," Catherine said, tilting her head to the left as she gazed at him, "but you have to move on, William."

"Move on?" he asked, his brows knitting together. A cold feeling erupted in his stomach.

"It's not your time yet," she said, placing her

other hand on his cheek, "but don't spend it alone. Find love again."

William adamantly shook his head. "No, Catherine, you are my love. There won't be another. Bounty hunting has become my life now."

"That is no life," Catherine said with a small smile. "You need to live, and you need to open your eyes."

As the words left her mouth, the sun grew brighter and the green grass faded away. Catherine slipped backwards out of his touch. William reached out for her, but she was always just out of his reach, until she too disappeared. He awoke with a gasp and a stinging pain descended.

The throbbing in his neck was so pronounced, he felt as if he could see the beat of it in his head, and there was a stiffness where his neck met his shoulder, keeping him from being able to move his head.

The wood planks he could see were unfamiliar to him, and his hand felt instinctively for his gun but came up empty.

"Easy now," a female voice said, and a pretty face entered his view. Blond locks circled her heart-shaped face and complemented her green eyes. "You were shot, and my father isn't sure he got all the shards out. You need to stay still and let your wound heal. There may still be fragments close to your neck."

Shot? The previous night flashed into William's mind and he jerked again, trying to sit up.

"No, you have to stay still," the woman insisted, pushing firmly on his chest to keep him down.

He stopped struggling. The pain was too great to continue anyway. Instead he swallowed to wet his throat and asked, "Did they get Monroe?" His voice came out hoarse and barely more than a whisper.

"The cattle thief?" the woman asked.

With deliberate effort, William nodded. Though painful, he found he could move his head if he did it slowly.

"Yes, they got him. Nellie too. It turns out she is his cousin."

With a small sigh, William relaxed against the pillow. At least his mark hadn't escaped though he probably wouldn't get the full bounty for him since local law enforcement had been forced to step in.

"I'm Mrs. Stewart," the woman continued, "and my father is Doc Moore. We're going to be taking care of you while you heal. Do you have any family we should notify?"

William moved his head the little he could. The

only family he had was the rapidly fading memory of the dream of Catherine.

"Oh, I'm sorry to hear that," Mrs. Stewart said, her face clouding with sympathy. "Well, rest for now. I'll be with you all day, so just ring this if you need me." She held up a little silver bell for him to see and then placed it near his right hand, folding his hand around the bell.

William started at the feel of her touch on his bare hand. How long had it been since a woman's gentle touch had affected him? Too quickly the warmth of her hand left his, and he was left alone with his thoughts. He wasn't generally the worrying type, but what if this injury halted his career? What would he do then?

There was nothing for him back in Barefoot Glen anymore. It was one reason he had accepted the Bounty Hunter proposition. He had loved serving as a deputy, but after Catherine had been killed by a stray bullet during his watch, life had lost its meaning. At least the money from collecting bounties filled part of the void in his heart, but if this injury kept him from performing his duties, he didn't know what he would do.

CHAPTER FOUR

E mma stole another glance at the man lying on the cot. He was handsome with his dark hair and chiseled features, so she had trouble believing he had no family. What had made him choose such a solitary life as being a bounty hunter?

She grabbed the towels from the washbasin and headed for the back door, grabbing the washboard and a bar of soap on the way. A water pump and a bucket sat just outside for her to wash the clinic's laundry and fill the wash basin when needed.

Emma pulled up the nearby stool and began priming the pump until the water flowed out and filled the bucket. She stuck the washboard in the bucket and began scrubbing the still pink towels.

"Well, hello, Emma. I hear you have a bounty hunter in your care."

Emma sighed at Carl's voice. They had grown up together and courted for a time until Joseph had come into her life. Carl had not so graciously stepped aside when it became clear her affections lay with the other man, but since Joseph's death, he had begun coming around again in hopes of a second chance with Emma. The problem was she had no interest in him.

"Yes, Carl, we do. He was shot last night, and he needs his rest, so I hope you weren't thinking of bothering him."

"Bothering? I'm never a bother, Emma, you should know that." He leaned against the back post just a few feet from her.

Right, never a bother. "What can I do for you, Carl?" Emma asked, using the soap to take her aggravation for Carl out on the towels.

"I wanted to see if you would like to come riding with me tomorrow?"

"Oh, I don't think I can, Carl. I've got this patient, and I promised Pa I'd help him out."

"It would just be for a few hours, Emma. Surely Doc Moore can handle the clinic for a few hours."

"He probably could," her father's voice interrupted the conversation and Emma glanced gratefully at him, "but I've been called to Opdyke West tomorrow for a few days, so Emma will have to take care of our guest on her own. I'm afraid riding will have to wait."

"Understood, sir." Carl had the decency to answer and nod politely before walking away.

"Thank you, Pa," Emma said as she pulled the towel out of the bucket. It wasn't as white as it had once been, but she felt sure it was as clean as it was going to get. She stood and placed it over the railing to begin drying before grabbing another towel.

"You're welcome," her father said, "but I was stating the truth. I'm going to check on our guest and make sure he can be moved. It would make me feel better for you to watch him at the homestead than to stay at the clinic overnight. I know Samuel is old enough, but I always feel better with you at home to watch out for the little ones."

"Do you think he can be moved?" Emma asked, concern coloring her voice. "He could barely speak to me earlier."

"He's stiff and sore, but I think if we get some men to help us load him in a wagon and unload him at the house that he'll be fine. However, I'm going to perform an examination to be sure."

Emma nodded as her father went back in the clinic. The stranger was going to be in their home for the foreseeable future. She wasn't sure how she felt about that, but it did make sense if her father were going to be gone. This way she could monitor the stranger and help out her siblings at home.

She finished washing the other towels and then brought them and the washboard inside. In one of the back rooms, a line of string had been strung across the room to serve as a clothesline. Emma draped the towels over the line before continuing to the main room.

"Ah, Emma, just in time," her father said. "I've examined Mr. Cook here, and while he still has a long road of healing, I do believe he is able to travel. I'm going to find a few able-bodied men and a wagon, and I shall return."

"I hear you're to be my private nurse," Mr. Cook said in a hoarse whisper after her father left.

Emma felt a heat sprout up her neck. "I will be your primary caretaker, but I assure you there will be nothing private about it. My father is bringing you to our homestead, and I have four younger brothers and sisters ranging in age from six to twenty."

The man blanched slightly before asking, "I don't suppose I have much choice, do I?"

With a smile, Emma shook her head. "I'm afraid not. My father is quite stubborn once he's made up his mind, and since he has been called to another town for a few days, he feels this is the most prudent course of action. Unfortunately, some of the smaller towns around here don't have a doctor in town and have to send for Pa. You're lucky you didn't get shot in one of those towns."

"I suppose you're right," he said with a slight smile, "but won't your husband mind you being away from him for so long?"

"My husband is deceased," Emma said softly.

"Oh, I'm sorry," he mumbled.

"Thank you. Well, you appear to be feeling a little better after your rest," Emma added, changing the conversation's direction.

"I'm a fast healer," Mr. Cook said, "though I'd be lying if I said I wasn't feeling any pain. My neck still feels as if it's on fire and my throat is parched."

"I could get you some water if you'd like," Emma offered.

"I'd like that," Mr. Cook said, and Emma scurried to the back room to grab a metal cup and fill it with water from the pump.

When she returned, her brow furrowed as she questioned how best to give him the drink. Her father had said he shouldn't move much, but she would need to sit him up a little or the water might choke him.

She set the cup down on the nearby table and perched on the edge of the cot. "This is probably going to hurt a bit, but I'm going to need to lift your head, so you can drink."

"I can handle the pain," he said, but she saw a flicker of fear in his green eyes.

As gingerly as she could, Emma slid her arm under his neck and pulled upwards. She saw him flinch and a low moan escaped his lips, but she was able to get him up enough to drink. He downed half of the liquid in the cup before signaling he was through.

After placing the cup back on the table, Emma lowered him back to the cot and removed her arm, but not before a tingling sensation flooded her arm. The sensation wasn't new to her, of course, but why was she feeling it for this stranger?

Emma glanced at Mr. Cook, but his eyes were closed, and his chest rose and fell in a labored pattern as if that had been more painful than he was letting on. If a mere drink caused this much pain, how was she going to get him to eat? He'd probably have to live on broth and soup for a few days until the pain became more manageable.

As she stood, the door of the clinic opened, and her father entered with Deputy Jennings and Mr. Brown, the owner of the mercantile.

"Good news, Mr. Cook," her father said, "Mr. Brown here has a long wooden board we can use as a stretcher for the trip. If we tie your head and feet to the board, it should limit the movement and save you a great deal of pain."

"Pa, just lifting him to give him a drink a moment ago caused him a great deal of pain. Are you sure moving him is wise?" Emma whispered in her father's ear. She didn't want to question his decision in front of the other men.

He patted her hand. "Don't worry, my dear. It will be fine."

Emma watched helplessly as the wooden plank was brought in. It was balanced across a stool and held in place by her father as Deputy Jennings hooked his arm under Mr. Cook's and Mr. Brown took his feet.

On the count of three, they hoisted Mr. Cook onto the plank, eliciting another small groan from the man. Then her father began wrapping bandages around Mr. Cook's head and the top of the board and then around his feet and the bottom of the board.

When the wrapping was finished, the two men lifted the stretcher and Emma and her father followed them out of the clinic. Her father took a moment to lock the door before asking, "Emma, why don't you and I ride in the back of the wagon with Mr. Cook to help keep him from being jostled."

"Yes, Pa," Emma said before climbing into the back of the wagon. Mr. Cook's eyes were still closed, and wrinkled lines marred his forehead letting her know he was still in pain.

Her father climbed up across from her and between the two of them, they managed to keep the stretcher relatively still on the short ride to their house.

"Emma, go and make up my bed for Mr. Cook here," her father instructed as the wagon came to a stop in front of the house. "And see if you can keep the children occupied with something until we get him comfortable."

Emma nodded and climbed down from the wagon, careful not to disturb Mr. Cook and cause him any more pain. As she reached the porch steps, the door swung open and Jennie ran out.

"You're home early. Does that mean we get to

play?" Jennie danced from one foot to the other in excitement.

"Maybe in a bit. I need to get father's bed made for a guest who will be staying with us," Emma said, patting her sister on the head before stepping by her.

"Who's our guest?" Jennie asked pulling on Emma's skirt as she followed her into the house.

"His name is Mr. Cook. He is a bounty hunter who was shot and needs us to look after him for a few days."

"He was shot?" Benjamin asked with interest, looking up from the kitchen table where he was studying.

"Yes, but you are not going to bother him," Emma admonished. "He is going to need his rest."

"Aw, shucks," Benjamin grumbled under his breath, but he dropped his eyes back to his paper.

Emma pushed open the door to her father's room. He was rarely home except to sleep, so there was very little out of place. She quickly smoothed the sheets and plumped the pillow before turning back to the door where she ran right into Jennie, who had been watching her every move.

"Is he handsome?" the young girl asked.

"What?" Emma asked as she stepped around the girl again.

"The guest. Is he handsome?" Jennie pressed again.

"I suppose," Emma said. She had noticed his chiseled features and his intriguing green eyes, but she had been more concerned with caring for him than noticing if he were handsome.

"Would you marry him?" Jennie asked in a sing-song voice stopping Emma in her tracks.

She whirled on the girl, her blond hair flying out behind her. "There will be no talk of marriage. He is a guest in our house to get better, not to get fixed up with someone." Emma felt a little guilt over her words when Jennie's face dropped. "I'm sorry, Jennie. Why don't you see if Benjamin needs any help with his studying?"

The little girl pouted her lip but did as she was asked. With a sigh, Emma resumed her task of returning to the wagon waiting outside. "Okay, Pa, your bed is ready."

The men moved into action. Her father climbed down from the back and Deputy Jennings and Mr. Brown hopped down from the front. They inched the stretcher out until they were able to each take an end. With her father holding the middle to keep it as still as possible, the men walked with a steady gait into the house and to her father's room.

Emma noticed that Mr. Cook's eyes remained closed though she wasn't sure if it was by choice or if he had simply passed out again. The men placed the stretcher on the side of the bed and then as before lifted Mr. Cook by the armpits and the feet to place him on the bed. As no groan accompanied this move, Emma assumed he had lost consciousness. She grabbed a nearby blanket and pulled it over him before following the men out of the room and shutting the door behind her.

"Thank you both," her father said to the other two men as they exited the front door. "Benjamin," he said turning to her brother, "Go find Samuel and hitch up my wagon please."

"Where are you going, Pa?" Jennie asked in a timid voice.

"To Opdyke West for a few days," her father answered. "Emma will be in charge. Where's Carrie?"

"Here, Pa," Carrie said emerging from the bedroom the girls shared.

"Carrie, can you take over cooking dinner for the next few days? Emma may have her hands full with our guest."

"Of course, Pa."

"Good, now Emma, listen carefully. You'll need to

monitor his heart rate often to make sure he isn't going into shock. Change the dressing once a day, but otherwise keep it covered to keep germs out. His neck will be sore, but he should be able to sit propped up, and he'll probably need soup or broth for a day or two but then get him on soft food. As soon as he's able, get him walking around."

Emma nodded, trying to memorize his instructions before asking, "What if he goes into shock, Pa?"

"Keep him comfortable, cover him with a blanket, and send Samuel to get me."

Emma nodded as the door opened and Samuel and Benjamin stepped inside. "The wagon's ready, Pa," Samuel said.

"Good, help out your sisters while I'm gone and keep an eye on the stranger. The shotgun is by the front door," her father said. He hugged each of them before exiting.

Emma exhaled and sent up a silent prayer that everything would be okay while her father was gone.

CHAPTER FIVE

Though the throbbing in his neck had lessened, the pain in William's stomach had now replaced it. He was hungry. His hand reached for the silver bell, but it wasn't there. A few further pats of the area near his hand yielded no result either. Where was the woman? In fact, where was he?

William's neck was still stiff, but he could tell from what he could see that the room was different, homier. The previous events flooded back into his mind. They had moved him from the clinic to the doctor's house. How long had he been out?

The door opened, and the blond woman entered carrying a tray with a bowl and a cup on it. "Oh, good, you're awake," she said upon seeing him. "I brought you some soup my sister Carrie made and some water. Do you feel up to eating?"

His stomach felt up to much more than just soup, but he wasn't sure how his neck would feel when he tried to sit up. "I'm starving," he said.

The woman smiled - what was her name again- and set the tray on a nearby table. As she reached behind him to move the pillow up, the sweet scent of vanilla and sugar filled his senses. Trying to ignore the tempting smell, William pushed against the bed and struggled to sit up. With a great deal of pain and a minor amount of groaning on his part, he managed to sit upright.

"Are you in too much pain?" the woman asked, her face scrunched in sympathy.

"It's fine," William said through clenched teeth. Stewart! That was her name, Mrs. Stewart.

"My father recommended just soup for a few days to make sure your wound is mostly healed before you do a lot of chewing, but I promise it's good soup."

"Thank you, Mrs. Stewart," he said, taking the soup bowl from her.

A soft pink flooded her cheeks. "I think, since you'll be staying with us for the next few days, that you can call me Emma."

William brought the bowl to his lips and managed

a large gulp before lowering it and stating, "Then you can call me Bill."

Emma's nose scrunched, and her face contorted with a look of displeasure. "Bill? Is that your full name?"

"No, it's William," he said. "You don't like Bill?"

"It sounds like an outlaw's name. If it's all the same, I will call you by your God-given name of William."

William stared at the woman. He should be offended, but he detected no ill will in her statement, and he rather liked the way William rolled off her tongue. "That's fine," he said and brought the bowl to his lips to hide his smile.

Though it still hurt to swallow, it was manageable pain and William quickly finished the bowl of soup and the water. "Would it be possible to get some more?" he asked as the roaring in his stomach was barely abated.

Emma's eyebrows inched up her forehead. "I see you've gotten your appetite back. Yes, I'll get you some more but first I need to change your dressing."

"Fine," he said with a nod. He didn't tell her that the thought of her gentle touch sent his heart beating faster.

As Emma leaned over him, he could see tiny

flecks of gold in her green eyes and he was drawn to them like he hadn't been since Catherine. Catherine - the image of her bleeding out in the street filled his mind. Even though he'd been a deputy sheriff, he hadn't been able to protect her. He pushed thoughts of Catherine and Emma out of his mind; he didn't need that pain again and she needed a man who could protect her.

Emma pulled back the dressing, and a grimace crossed her face. She tried to recover and quickly averted her eyes, but William had seen the shock in her eyes.

"Is it bad?" William asked.

"No," Emma said biting her lip. She was not a good liar, but he found the gesture endearing none-theless. "I just haven't treated a lot of gunshot wounds."

Based on her reaction, he wondered if she had treated any gunshot wounds. "Have you always helped your father out?" William asked, trying to keep his mind off Emma's perfect pink lips as she cleaned the wound.

"No, I don't mind helping people, but I really just wanted to be a mother and raise a family."

She touched a sensitive area of the wound and William sucked in his breath. Her eyes grew wide.

"I'm sorry. Does it hurt too badly?"

"It's better today than it was yesterday," he said as the pain subsided.

As Emma turned to grab another bandage, William fought the urge to ask her why she didn't have a family. He was not a great judge of age but guessed her to be in her mid-twenties. Most women were married by twenty-one in the West.

Though curious, he knew he hadn't known her long enough to ask such a personal question. Thankfully, she finished her story, satisfying his curiosity.

"I was married but my husband was killed shortly after we married. After Joseph's death, I moved back in with my father and began helping him in the clinic."

"Do you," William paused, but his intrigue got the best of him and though he wasn't sure why he cared, he held his breath as he finished the question, "hope to marry again?"

She tilted her head and narrowed her eyes at him.

"I'm sorry," he said. "That was too forward of me to ask."

"No, it's fine. It's just that my sister asked the same thing yesterday. It's like everyone is trying to marry me off all of a sudden." She began applying the new dressing as she spoke. "I hope one day to marry again if God sees fit to send me the right man. I'm in no hurry though. I learned a long time ago to wait for His timing."

William bit the inside of his lip to keep his comments to himself. He had once invested as much stock in God as Emma seemed to, but the loss of Catherine had shaken his faith and he was no longer sure God existed. Worse yet, William wasn't sure he cared whether God existed or not.

"Okay, all done. I'll go and get you more soup now."

As Emma left the room, William leaned farther back into the pillow and closed his eyes. He had been hiding the pain from her, but the throbbing sensation was starting to pulse into his head.

"Were you really shot?"

He opened his eyes to see a young boy with dirty blond hair and an even younger girl with dark brown hair staring at him. These must be the younger siblings. "Yes, I was, but your sister just changed the dressing, so I can't show you."

"Did it hurt?" the little girl asked, her blue eyes wide and round.

William chuckled. "I can't recommend it. It's definitely painful."

"Are you really a bounty hunter?" the boy asked.

"Yes, I am, but again I can't recommend it. It is how I got shot after all."

"Benjamin, Jennie, get out of here and leave our guest alone," Emma scolded, re-entering the room with another serving of soup.

"It's okay," William said. "They were just being curious."

"Yes, well, they are supposed to be doing their chores, which is what they are going to do now." Under her admonishing stare, the two younger children ducked their heads and scurried out of the room. "I'm sorry. They're not used to having visitors in the house."

"How many of you are there?" William asked. He thought she had mentioned the number once, but the previous day was still cloudy from the pain he had been in.

"Five," Emma answered, passing him the bowl. "I'm the oldest and Jennie is the youngest at six. I'm sure you'll meet Carrie and Samuel, the older two, soon enough."

William downed the second bowl of soup and then handed it back to Emma. "Did your father say how long I would need to stay here?"

Emma smiled at him. "Are you tired of our hospitality already?"

"No, it's not that," William said quickly, "but I still need to bring Monroe in to collect my bounty."

"Do you enjoy it?" Emma's voice had dropped to little more than a whisper. "Being a bounty hunter?"

"It pays well," William said.

"But isn't it lonely?" Emma continued. "Don't you want more out of life than that?"

"No. With more comes pain, and I've had enough of that to last a lifetime."

Emma bit her lip as if she wanted to say more, but his tone of voice had cut her questions short. He was glad. He didn't feel like talking about the pain. Burying it and ignoring it was much easier, and though Emma had also lost a spouse, he doubted she had held her husband as she watched the life slip out of his eyes as he had with Catherine.

"I'll be back later with supper," Emma said, heading for the door. "You should get your rest."

"Wait, do you know where my horse is?" William asked. "I had her tied up at the saloon when I went after Monroe, and I have items in my saddle bag I'd like back."

"I'm not sure," Emma replied, "but I'll send Samuel to look. If he finds your horse, he can bring her back to our barn and board her until you're feeling better."

"Thank you." A part of William wanted to call her back, so he could explain about his pain, but he kept his mouth shut. It was better this way. He didn't need to be distracted by Emma's pretty face, and she didn't need the likes of him in her life.

CHAPTER SIX

As Emma closed her father's door and meandered into the kitchen to wash the bowl, she wondered what pain William held in his past. At only twenty-five, she had seen enough people suffer through tragedy to recognize the signs. Her own father had displayed similar signs when their mother died, throwing himself into his work and forgetting his family for a time.

Was that what had happened to William? It would make sense. He appeared to be in his early thirties and most men were married by that time. He certainly was handsome enough to have had a wife.

Emma shook her head at that thought. She had no business noticing his handsome features. William Cook was not going to remain in her life. He would be gone as soon as he was healed. He had made that evident just a moment ago. And she could never be a bounty hunter's wife. She had worried too much when Joseph was with the Rangers and then had been forced to deal with his early death.

No, while she knew safety was not guaranteed in the West, she needed someone stable. Someone who would want to ranch or farm or do something less dangerous. Someone like... Carl. Emma sighed as she sat at the kitchen table. Only she had no affection for Carl, and after having a marriage to Joseph based on affection, she wasn't sure she could settle for anything less in the future.

The family Bible sitting at the edge of the table caught her eye and Emma pulled it closer to her. Without knowing what specifically she was looking for, she flipped open the large book landing in the book of John.

An underlined verse jumped out at her. *Peace I leave with you, My peace I give to you; not as the world giveth, give I unto you. Let not your heart be troubled, neither let it be afraid. - John 14:27*. Yes, that's what she needed to do. She needed to give her troubles over to God. He had always been there for her, even when she lost Joseph and felt alone. In fact, it had been then she had felt closest to God, almost as if she could feel His loving arms around her and His fatherly voice telling her it would be okay.

"What cha doing?"

Jennie's voice broke through Emma's thoughts, and she opened her eyes and smiled at her sister. "I was just talking to God."

"For the man?" Jennie asked.

"William?" Emma asked, confused. "No, more for myself really."

"William, is it?" Carrie asked, entering from the girls' bedroom. That girl had a knack for hearing her name in conversations or entering the room whenever she thought she might learn something juicy.

Emma shook her head in protest even as she felt heat climb up her neck. "It's not like that. He's just going to be here a few days, and it felt silly to keep calling him Mr. Cook."

"Of course it did," Carrie said. "It's much harder to entertain a fantasy if you constantly have to refer to him by his last name."

"Speaking from experience? You should know," Emma teased back. "I've seen the way you look at Phillip Alder in church."

This time Carrie's cheeks turned scarlet. "That's not the same thing at all," she protested.

"Oh isn't it?" Emma said with a laugh.

"You're both carrying torches," Jennie shouted and pointed a finger at them.

Emma and Carrie exchanged a wicked glance and then turned their attention on poor Jennie. "Let's get her," Carrie said, and the two older girls began to tickle Jennie until she squealed and they all fell on the floor in a heap of laughter.

CHAPTER SEVEN

W hen William woke later in the day, the room was much darker. Someone had lit a small oil lamp on the table near the bed, Emma probably. William wondered when she would be coming in again. His stomach still rumbled with hunger.

He wondered if he should holler for her or try to get out of bed himself, but after struggling to pull himself to a sitting position, he gave up and leaned back against the pillow. It wasn't that the pain was intolerable. Oh, it was still bad when he moved but manageable; the real problem was the lack of food had made him dizzy. The room had begun spinning as soon as he tried to move to the edge of the bed.

"I have dinner," Emma said, entering as if she had read his mind.

"Is it more than soup this time?" William asked over another growl from his stomach. "I'm starving."

"It's a stew," Emma answered with a smile. "Carrie put in some vegetables but softened them up for you."

William hoped it would be enough. Emma set the bowl on the table and then returned to help William sit up. Though still painful, he enjoyed the soft touch of her skin and the sweet smell of her as she leaned near.

When he was upright, she handed him the bowl and spoon. "Samuel found your horse. She's in our barn now and he brought in your saddle bag," she said pointing to his bag which lay on the floor against the far wall.

"Thank you," he said after swallowing a large mouthful of the warm stew.

"You're welcome," she said. She glanced toward the door, then pursed her lips and frowned. Turning her face back to him, she asked, "Would you like me to read to you? You must be awfully bored laying in here all alone."

William wondered if she were asking simply out of kindness or if there was some attraction on her part, but he found he didn't care. He liked her voice, and he didn't want to be alone.

"I'd like that," he said as he spooned up another bite. The carrots and potatoes had been cooked to a tee and required very little chewing on his part which helped with the pain.

Her eyes lit up and a dimple appeared in her cheek as she smiled. "Wonderful. I'll be right back." With a light step, she exited the room, returning a moment later with a large black book under her arm.

William paled when he realized what the book was. He should have asked what she wanted to read to him as he wasn't really in the mood for the Bible.

"Are you a fan of the Psalms?" she asked as she pulled over the wooden chair and sat down.

"I used to be," William said. It wasn't a complete lie; he and Catherine had often read the Psalms together. He had enjoyed them then, but he hadn't picked up a Bible since her death.

Emma raised an eyebrow at him as if unsure if she should continue, but when William offered no further objection, she opened the Bible and began to read.

Her voice was low and melodious, and William found himself enjoying the reading in spite of the subject matter. Before he knew it, the stew was gone, and while he wasn't completely full, it had satisfied the immediate gnawing hunger.

Emma finished Psalm 121 and closed the book. "You know, you are a miracle. If that bullet had hit anywhere else, you would probably be dead. God must have had an angel watching out for you. Is there anything else I can get you tonight?"

"No, I think I'm good for tonight," William answered though he was tempted to ask for another bowl of stew.

"Alright then," she said standing and taking the bowl from him. "Rest well, and I'll be back in the morning to check on you."

William lay back and pondered her words. He knew surviving a gunshot wound in general wasn't always a guarantee and especially one so near the neck. Could it be true that God was watching out for him? But if so, why? He certainly hadn't been giving God any of his time or attention.

CHAPTER EIGHT

E mma placed the Bible on the table and washed the bowl in the sink. As the water swirled in the bowl, her mind wandered to William again. Though he had let her read, she had seen him tense at the sight of the Bible and had caught his vague answer about the Psalms. She wondered what hurt in his past had driven him from God's loving arms.

"Emma, will you read me a story before bed?" Jennie asked, entering the room. Her long brown hair hung around her shoulders and her hand-me-down nightgown touched the floor.

"Of course. Why don't you gather everyone else and we'll all read together?"

Jennie smiled, nodded, and raced away to gather

her brothers and sister. Emma dried the bowl and set it beside the sink. Would she ever have her own children to read to? She loved her siblings, but it wasn't the same.

"God, if you see fit," she whispered, "I'd love another chance at a family. Please help me be patient and wait on your timing."

A moment later, Jennie returned followed by Benjamin, Carrie, and Samuel. Emma grabbed the Bible again and sat in the middle of the couch. The two youngest sat on either side of her and Carrie and Samuel perched on the arms of the couch.

Emma flipped the pages of the Bible, thinking about what story to read. A memory from long ago when Carrie was just a baby flashed into her mind. Their mother had still been alive then, a vibrant young woman with dark hair and crystal blue eyes. She had often read to them at night and Emma's favorite story had always been the birth of Jesus. Though not Christmas or Easter, she flipped to the back of the book and began to read the story of Mary.

When she finished, Jennie was asleep on her lap and Benjamin's eyes were heavy.

"I'll get him," Samuel said, scooping up his little

brother and heading to the back room the boys shared.

Emma did the same with Jennie, grunting a little under the weight. While not a large child, she had grown tall enough to be awkward in Emma's arms. She followed Carrie into the room they shared and laid Jennie in the large bed.

It was a tight squeeze with all three of them in the bed, but Emma didn't often mind. She liked having her sisters near her, and after Joseph's death, she found no enjoyment in sleeping alone. Her own eyes closed soon after she heard Carrie's breath slow and become rhythmic.

CHAPTER NINE

W illiam awoke when the sun's light broke through the window. He was tired of lying in bed, and he was bored. The need to do something, *anything*, burned in his veins, and while the pain hadn't gone away entirely, he believed it had dulled enough that he could try moving.

Remembering to take it slower this time after yesterday's fiasco, he dropped his right leg out of the bed first before pushing up with his arms. He had just achieved a sitting position with one leg out of the bed when Emma entered the room.

"What are you doing?" she gasped, hurrying toward him and placing the tray she was holding on the table. "You're supposed to be resting." She faced him with her hands on her hips and an reproachful look on her face.

The look was comical on her, but William swallowed his laughter, sure she would take offense to it. "I can't lay in this bed another whole day," he said instead. "Please, just let me see if I can handle moving around."

Her bottom lip folded under in that endearing gesture again, and he could see the indecision in her eyes.

"If it hurts too much, I promise I'll get back in bed," he pleaded.

"Alright, if you promise," she said and held out a hand to help him up.

He grasped her slender hand, ignoring the sensation that shot up his arm, and used her weight as leverage to swing his other leg out of the bed and push himself up. The pain in his neck throbbed a little but wasn't unbearable. Unfortunately, he had stood up too quickly and black dots encroached his vision. He felt himself start to sway.

"Whoa," Emma's voice said, and her arms wrapped around his chest to stabilize him.

William's body reacted impulsively to a woman being in his arms again and his own arms circled her. The smell of vanilla and sugar filled his nose.

When the room stopped spinning, William registered how perfectly Emma fit in his arms. His heart sped up and his gaze dropped to Emma's face. Her green eyes met his, filled with desire and confusion. Her perfect pink lips parted, and she inhaled. William wanted to kiss her, to taste those lips, but before he could say or do anything, she stepped out of his embrace, averting her eyes and breaking the moment.

"I think you need more rest," she said as she turned away from him and fiddled with something on the tray. He couldn't help but feel pleased at the pink blush on her cheeks. She must have felt something too.

"Nonsense," he said, clearing his throat to hide the emotions he was feeling. "I'm fine now. I just need to remember to stand more slowly next time."

"In that case, would you care to eat breakfast at the table with the rest of us?" Emma asked.

"I would sure like to try," William said.

With a nod, Emma picked up the tray and led the way to the homey kitchen. The table was already filled with the younger brother and sister he had already met as well as an elder boy and girl he had yet to meet.

"Carrie, can you set another place for our guest?" Emma asked.

A girl who appeared to be a younger version of Emma pushed her chair back and walked into the kitchen, returning a moment later with a plate and utensils. She set the plate down across from the only other empty setting at the table.

"You've already met Benjamin and Jennie," Emma said pointing at the two youngest children who were shoving pancakes in their mouths. "The other two are Samuel and Carrie."

Carrie flashed him a small smile while Samuel nodded his head at William. Emma put the bowl of porridge she had brought from the bedroom at the place setting Carrie had just laid down. While the porridge looked delicious, William's stomach rumbled at the sight and smell of the pancakes.

"If you think you can handle it, you are welcome to try some pancakes," Emma said as if reading his mind. She pulled out the chair across from him and sat down.

With a sheepish grin, William sat at the table and stabbed two pancakes with his fork. He forced himself to cut the pancakes into smaller bites though all he wanted to do was shove the entire thing in and fill the gaping hole in his belly. The act of chewing put a little more strain on the wound, but he found he could tolerate the pain, and before he knew it, the two original pancakes were gone. Along with two others he had for seconds.

As he finished chewing the last bite, he looked up to see Emma staring at him, a bemused expression on her face.

"Guess I was hungry," he said with a half smirk and a shrug of his shoulders.

"I guess you were," she said with a laugh. "I'm glad you were able to join us for breakfast, but I think you need to get back to bed now."

"Nonsense," William said. "I need to walk around. My neck and shoulders are stiff, but my legs work fine, and I'm certain your father said I would need exercise when I was feeling better."

As Emma bit her bottom lip, William knew he had struck gold. Their gazes locked, and William's heart did another stutter step in his chest. Before it could really ramp up, Jennie's voice broke the connection.

"You can go, Emma. I'll help Carrie clean up." Jennie ended this statement with a giant wink at Emma which caused a lovely pink to bloom on Emma's porcelain cheeks.

"Yes, we can get this," Carrie spoke up in a similar teasing tone.

William had to bite his lips to keep from smiling

not only at the girls' antics but also at the clueless faces of their brothers.

"Very well then, but we'll keep it short. Shall we, William?" Emma stood and smoothed her skirt before raising her head to meet his eyes.

"We shall," he said, following her lead.

CHAPTER TEN

E mma couldn't believe how her sisters had embarrassed her, but she also couldn't deny the excitement she felt about showing William the town. Would it be possible he could fall in love with it and decide to stay?

"What would you like to see?" she asked as they stepped onto the porch. The morning sun was warm, but not hot yet, and a light breeze rustled the leaves of the trees. "I don't want you out for long since it's your first bit of exercise."

"Why don't you show me one of your favorite spots?" William asked.

Emma's brow wrinkled in thought. What were her favorite spots? The church for sure. Maybe the large lavender Crape Myrtle tree she had often liked to read under when she was younger. And of course, the sage fields. No one should miss their majestic bloom.

"Alright, I'll take you through downtown to one of my favorite spots. That way you can see the rest of the town on the way, but if you get tired and need to rest, be sure to let me know. My father would have my hide if I had you out and about too soon and caused damage."

A playful smile pulled at William's lips. "I promise to be a model patient, Nurse, and tell you when I need a rest."

Emma blushed at the tone in William's voice. Was he simply teasing her, or could there be feelings behind his words?

She led the way off the porch and towards town. Doc Moore's house was on the opposite side of town from the saloon and Emma was happy to be able to avoid the place. Not only was it a morally decrepit den, but she figured William wouldn't enjoy a reminder of his injury there.

On their side of town was the schoolhouse, a large building that at this point still held only one room, but Emma had heard the men in town talking about the need to build a separation in the room. "This is our schoolhouse," Emma said. "It's quiet today as it's Saturday, but I really don't know how Margaret Goodman keeps up with all the children. It can be awfully noisy during lunch time."

"I bet," William said chuckling.

The church appeared next, it's white exterior gleaming in the sun. "This is one of my favorite places," Emma said to William. "I've always loved this building. It's like I feel God stands at the door welcoming us each week." Emma noticed that William glanced quickly at the building and then away. Again, she wondered what pain had distanced him from God.

"This is the cafe," Emma said as they neared the next establishment. "We don't often eat here as it is too expensive to feed a family of six, but Pa took us once for a special treat. And, the food is excellent." Her smile froze on her face though when Carl exited the restaurant and looked up at them.

"Oh, so too busy to ride with me, but not too busy to show some stranger around our town?" Carl asked with a sneer.

"Carl, this is Mr. Cook, the man who was shot. He felt up to some exercise today, so I am merely allowing him a supervised walk," Emma said with a small sigh. "Not that it's any of your business."

"Mr. Cook, huh?" Carl asked turning his attention to William. "The Bounty Hunter, right? Are you planning on sticking around once you heal?"

William stared at Carl. "I am not. I have to turn Monroe into the authorities and then I'm sure I'll have more jobs to attend to, though as Mrs. Stewart said, I'm not sure how that is any of your business."

Carl narrowed his eyes at William. "Let's just say I have a vested interest in your leaving." He flashed a smile at Emma before tapping the brim of his hat. "I'll see you in church tomorrow, Emma."

Curling her hands into fists, Emma watched Carl walk away. He had once been a close friend, but he had no right to act as if he owned her.

"What's with him?" William asked when Carl was far enough away not to hear them.

With a shake of her head, Emma continued walking. "We courted for a time until I met Joseph. Now that I'm a widow, he thinks he has some claim on me."

"But you don't feel the same?" William asked.

Avoiding the question, Emma stated, "Come on." Turning down a side street, they headed to the outer part of town where the large lavender Crape Myrtle tree sat overlooking the creek.

"We aren't seeing the rest of downtown?" William asked.

"Short walk, remember? Plus, there are beautiful things in Sage Creek outside of downtown you should see as well."

William's brows pulled together in confusion, but he followed her, keeping his questions to himself.

The downtown buildings faded into smaller houses. When the tree came into sight, Emma heard William's intake of breath beside her. "Isn't it gorgeous?" she asked. It looked especially pretty today in full bloom with bright purple flowers covering the tips of the branches.

"It's a sight for sure," he said. "How long has this tree been here?"

"I'm not sure," Emma said, sitting down against the trunk. As the tree stood about twenty feet, it had a thick enough trunk to lean against. "As long as I've been here anyway. I used to love to come here and read in the afternoons." She patted the ground beside her in an invitation to sit.

William looked unsure at first, but finally managed to adjust his position enough that he appeared comfortable. In order to share the trunk, he had to sit quite close to Emma and she could feel the warmth radiating from him.

"You asked me about Carl," she said, returning to the previous conversation. "I might have married him once if I had never met Joseph. Carl is loyal and predictable, and I've known him since we were children, but I was never in love with him. Of course, out here, you don't often get to marry for love." Emma glanced at William before dropping her eyes to the blades of grass around her knee.

"Then one day, Joseph rode into town. He was strong and brave and daring, and he swept me off my feet." Her voice faded as she thought back to the day Joseph had proposed to her.

"Oh, my, that was so much fun, but could we take a short break?" Emma asked, fanning herself. "That last dance wore me out."

"Of course," Joseph said, taking her hand and leading her off the dance floor. He led the way to the hayloft where bales of hay were set up. After smoothing down the prickly pieces, Joseph laid his coat down for Emma to sit on.

When they were seated, he grabbed her hands. "I know it's only been a few months, Emma, but I was taken by you the first time I met you. I never thought I'd be one to stay in the same place for very long, but I can see a life with you here in Sage Creek."

Emma's breath caught in her throat. Was he about to propose?

"I've already asked your father, so now I'm officially asking you. Will you marry me, Emma Moore?"

Her heart soared as she nodded. "Of course I'll marry you."

The memory faded, and Emma glanced at William. "Though our marriage was short, it was full of love. When he died, I knew my prospects were slim. I suppose I could have stayed in the house Joseph built, but there were too many memories and it isn't always safe for a woman to be alone, especially at night.

"So, I had two choices. I could return to my father's house or marry another. Carl proposed to me the day after we buried Joseph, but I just couldn't do it. I may never find another marriage based on love, but I refuse to give up hope just yet."

A silence fell, and Emma looked at William from lowered lids. "Have you ever been married?" she asked, dropping her eyes back to the ground as the words left her lips.

"I was," he said. "Like your husband, she died too early."

He said nothing more, and Emma knew better than to push.

"What did your husband do, if you don't mind me asking," William said after a long pause.

"He was a member of the Texas Rangers," Emma replied. "I thought at first that sounded romantic, but I spent a lot of nights alone, and when he went out on his last job after some bandit named Holden, I worried every night. I just had a feeling that something was wrong. It turned out, I was right. Are you okay?" she asked noticing William's pale face.

"Yes, I'm fine," he said, turning his wide eyes from her. "I think I'm just getting a little tired. Could we continue the tour another time?"

"Of course," Emma said, adjusting her skirts and standing. Though he did look tired, his reaction had occurred so suddenly that Emma wondered if it were more from something she said. She replayed the conversation in her head as they walked back to the homestead, but she couldn't for the life of her figure out why he would be affected by her husband's death.

CHAPTER ELEVEN

W illiam woke before the sun. He had spent the rest of the afternoon the day before and most of the night trying to decide if he should tell Emma what he knew and if so, then how. He should have put the name together when she first mentioned her husband, but he had served with so many men. Neither Joseph nor Stewart was a highly unusual name, but when Emma mentioned John Holden, the details had come flashing back.

After Catherine's death, William had no longer felt he could serve the town of Barefoot Glen any longer. After all, if a deputy couldn't protect his own wife, what good was he? He had turned in his badge, packed up his horse, and headed for some place to clear his head. Where he had landed was Austin, Texas where Ben Wallace had sold him on the benefits of being a Texas Ranger.

With nothing tying him down, William had agreed and enjoyed riding with the other men until the day he was approached by Jack Hardesty.

"Are you Wild Bill Cook?"

William looked up at the visitor. He had been given the nickname a few months into becoming a Ranger as his fearless attitude became known, but he didn't recognize this man with his tan skin, dark hair, and a handlebar mustache.

"I am. What can I do for you?"

"Actually," the man said with a small smile, "it's more about what I can do for you."

"I don't understand," William said, shaking his head.

"Your reputation has preceded you, and I think you would make a great bounty hunter. I'm here to offer you a job."

"I already have a job," William said, dropping his gaze back to the desk.

"Yes, but I doubt it can pay like this." The man slid a paper across the desk and into William's gaze.

William had no real need for more money as he had no family to support and the Ranger pay was more than enough to cover his needs. But there was something about seeing all those zeros that grabbed his attention. His eyes widened as he read the information. "Four thousand dollars?"

The man nodded. "And that's just your cut; because this job is so big, a few of us are being called in. Normally you'd work alone and earn at least double that."

"What do you need me to do?" William asked, meeting the man's eyes again.

"You'll need to round up some good Rangers. We're wanting at least twenty men on this take down. John Holden is not one to underestimate."

And that was how Joseph Stewart had become involved. William had rounded up a few men from Austin and then sent out telegrams to surrounding areas. Joseph Stewart had been one of many who had thrown their hats in the ring.

The men knew going after outlaws was dangerous, but even William had had no idea how dangerous this one was. William wondered now why Stewart had joined. If the man had recently married why had he been willing to take on a job that might be dangerous? Had he needed the money? Being a Ranger didn't pay as well as bounty hunting, but it would have been a nice sum anyway. Perhaps it had been for the money or perhaps just the sense of duty.

William tightened his grip on the reins with one hand while the other sat on the hilt of his revolver. A glance around revealed the other men in a similar position. They had been tracking the infamous John Holden for days, and finally their undercover operative had told them Holden was on a train headed for Dallas.

That train now sat in front of them, stopped on the tracks by the deputies on board. Jack Hardesty, the leader of this roundup, had managed to get a few deputies on the train at the last station. Now the group outside was simply waiting for the sign that Holden had been apprehended.

A shot rang out in the air, and the men sprang into action. Several men dismounted and headed for the main door of the train with their guns drawn. A door towards the back of the train slid open, and a man jumped out.

"It's Horace Gilbert," one of the men shouted out. "Don't let him get away." Gilbert was Holden's right-hand man and just as bad as Holden.

William turned his horse that direction and motioned his Rangers to follow him. Gilbert had gotten a head start on them, but they were faster on horses and quickly saw him ducking through the tall sage grass.

Holding his arm as steady as he could, William fired off a shot. It missed but must have been close as Gilbert quickly shifted direction. A few more shots went off around William as the other men aimed and fired. None of them hit the mark either, but it was much harder to hit a running, zigzagging target.

Taking a deep breath, William focused his eyes on the suspect and fired another shot. This time Gilbert went down. By the time William reached the area, another Ranger was hauling him to his feet. His shot had hit Gilbert's shoulder, but it appeared to be just a flesh wound.

"Nice work, Cook," one of his Rangers said as he secured Gilbert's hands behind his back.

William nodded and tapped his hat. All in a day's work. He had always been a decent shot but had rarely used it until Catherine's death when a drunken brawl poured out into the streets. The bullet had hit her as she exited the mercantile, and William had watched as she fell, and the contents of her bag spilled into the street.

He turned his horse around and headed back to the train to make sure Holden had also been apprehended. William was almost to the train when he heard the gunfire behind him. Turning quickly, he saw Gilbert had managed to get a hand free and had grabbed the gun of one of the nearby Rangers. A bullet took Gilbert down, but not before William saw two of his men fall.

William raced back to the scene. Three of his men lay on the ground along with Gilbert, who had been shot in the chest.

"Sorry, boss," Henry, one of the Rangers he worked closely with in Austin said, "he managed to grab Joseph's gun and had him, Harry, and Arthur shot before we knew what happened."

William cursed his stupidity as he dismounted. He should have stayed to make sure Gilbert was secure before checking in on Holden. Harry Givens moaned on the ground. He'd taken a shot to the arm but would probably be okay. Arthur Jones and

Joseph Stewart lay still. As they were both men from other cities who had answered his call for help, William knew nothing about them.

"Load them all up," William ordered. "We can at least send their bodies home." He turned away before the emotion displayed on his face. This was his fault.

The door to the room banged open, shattering his walk down memory lane. Jennie raced into the room.

"You're not up yet?" she asked. "You have to get up. It's church day."

"Oh, I don't usually go to church," William said.

"Why not?" the little girl asked, her face scrunching in confusion.

"Well because God took something I loved," he replied.

Jennie stared at him. "So, you haven't felt like worshipping Him since?"

"That's right, I haven't," he said.

"I know how that feels," she said, dropping her eyes and twisting her foot into the floor. "Pastor Lewis always says that we might not choose or understand the things God allows, but we should trust His plan and continue to follow Him."

William stared at the doll-faced girl. Her blue eyes were innocent and childlike, so in contrast to the profound words that had just escaped her mouth. "How did you get so knowledgeable?" he asked.

"I had to talk with Pastor Lewis a lot when I realized Mommy died giving me life. That's a lot for a six-year-old to carry, you know?"

William bit his lip to keep from smiling at the girl. Her words were heartbreaking and not funny, but the seriousness in which she said them created a funny image in his head. "Yes, I can see how that would be a lot to carry," he said.

"Who did God take from you?" she asked.

He paused. Did he really want to re-open this wound? However, she had been brave enough to share about her mother, and she was only six, so he couldn't see the harm. "My wife. God took my wife from me."

"Come to church with me. You can sit beside me, and I'll ask God to give you the comfort He's given me."

Though William still had no desire to step into a church, he couldn't say no to the endearing face before him. "Okay, skedaddle out of here for a minute, so I can get cleaned up and I'll meet you outside."

A wide smile broke out on Jennie's face. "I'll tell Emma," she cried, "she'll be so pleased."

Before he could ask what she meant by that, Jennie had spun and raced out of the room as quickly as she entered. Still a little stiff, William walked slowly to his saddle bag and reached inside for a new change of clothes. The ones he was currently wearing were beginning to become ripe. He would have loved a bath as well, but there was no time for that. With new clothes on, he headed into the kitchen.

CHAPTER TWELVE

E
mma looked up in surprise when William entered. He hadn't seemed the church-going type and even though Jennie had said she had convinced him to come, Emma still hadn't believed it would happen. Plus, he was still healing. "Good morning."

"Morning," he said. "I guess I'm attending church with you if that's all right."

"Of course. Everyone is welcome in the house of the Lord. Would you like some breakfast? Carrie made some eggs and bacon."

"Sure, and I'll take some coffee if you have some."

Emma smiled as she loaded up a plate for him. "I'm not much of a partaker myself, but Samuel brews some every morning before feeding the animals." They didn't have a large farm, but a few chickens to supply their eggs, some hogs for ham, and of course horses. "There should be some left," she said, nodding at the carafe on the stove.

"I'll have some then. Is that where your siblings are now?" William asked looking around the room as he pulled out a chair and sat at the table.

Emma placed the plate in front of him before returning to the stove. "Yes, Samuel and Benjamin are finishing up their chores and Carrie is getting ready in our room." She poured the black liquid into a cup. "Do you take milk or sugar?"

"A dash of milk would be fine," William said.

Emma added it and returned to the table placing the steaming cup in front of William.

"Thank you," he said, catching her eye.

He held her gaze a moment longer than necessary and Emma felt her cheeks begin to burn. "That was nice of you to agree to attend church for Jennie's sake," she said, turning away to hide the effect he was having on her.

"Did she tell you why?" he asked as he lifted the cup to his lips.

Emma shook her head. "No, she simply said you agreed to come." William's eyebrow arched on his head as if he didn't believe her. "She may be only six, but she had to grow up quickly when she learned about Ma. In some ways, she's a lot older than she seems."

William opened his mouth to respond, but before he could, the two boys clomped into the house.

"The animals are fed," Benjamin said.

"No thanks to you," Samuel said, shooting his brother a look. "He almost fell in the mud trying to feed the hogs before I was ready."

"But I didn't," Benjamin said, pulling back his shoulders and puffing out his little chest.

"Alright boys," Emma said. "Enough arguing. Clean up. We'll be heading to church in a minute."

The next few minutes were a flurry of activity as Carrie and Jennie emerged from the girl's room, Emma put the left-out dishes in the sink to be washed upon their return, and the boys reappeared with combed hair and clean shirts.

"Okay, let's go," Emma said, ushering the crew outside. "Don't get dirty," she shouted to Jennie and Benjamin as they raced ahead.

"What kind of preacher is Pastor Lewis?" William asked, falling into step beside Emma. His face appeared pinched and anxious.

She glanced at him, wondering what the meaning

behind the question really was. "He's young but seems very knowledgeable. He speaks often on the love of God and having a true relationship with Him. I think you'll like him."

"Oh good," he said, visibly relaxing. "I was afraid he might be one of those fire and brimstone types and I wasn't sure I could handle it."

Emma laughed. "No, we haven't had one like that in a long time, and I'm glad. I think having a relationship with God is more important than trying to scare people into believing."

They arrived at the church and joined the other townspeople filing in. Emma waved at Sarah Miller as she sat next to Kate and Deputy Jennings. She caught the eye of a few of the other women in the town as she walked up the row to her family's pew. Unfortunately, she also managed to catch the eye of Carl, who glared at her when he caught sight of William behind her. Emma sighed softly. Would she never convince him he held no claim on her?

Emma sat down with Jennie on her left and William on her right. She wasn't sure who was the bigger wiggler. Jennie had the normal six-year-old wiggles, but William kept shifting in his seat, crossing and then uncrossing his leg, leaning forward and then leaning back. At least he finally seemed to relax when Pastor Lewis started speaking.

"I came this morning with a message prepared," Pastor Lewis began, "but I feel God telling me that someone here needs a different message. Maybe many of you. So, I hope you'll bear with me as I let God lead this message where He wants it to go." He paused for a moment as if gathering his thoughts.

"I had someone ask me this week," he continued, "if Heaven was as beautiful as you could imagine, if there was no sickness or physical ailments there, if you could rest and be reunited with loved ones, would you want to go?"

Of course, Emma thought to herself. *That is the point to Heaven, isn't it?*

"What if you could have all those things, but Jesus wasn't there?" Pastor Lewis continued. "What if you had to choose? You could have the perfect place of Heaven or you could follow Jesus. Would you still choose Jesus?"

A feeling of conviction settled on Emma. Though she knew the Bible said you got both, she had to wonder if she would choose Jesus if forced to make a choice. Heaven to her had always meant seeing her mother again and recently seeing Joseph again while Jesus had been the byproduct. Now, she realized she had her priorities backwards. She ought to be looking forward to seeing Jesus in Heaven and everything else should be a byproduct.

"I know you all love Jesus," Pastor Lewis continued, "or you probably wouldn't be here, but do you love Jesus for who he is? Or do you love Him for what you hope He will grant you? Are you tithing because God said we should or because you hope by tithing that God will increase your wealth? We all have moments of selfishness, just like James and John did in Mark chapter ten when they asked to sit at Jesus' right and left hands, but we must work through those moments and keep our vision on God.

"I have no doubt that when we get to Heaven, it will be beautiful and amazing and pain free, but I don't believe that will be because it's Heaven. I believe it will be that way because God will be there, and we will stand in awe of Him and wonder how we could have second guessed Him or put our faith in anything but Him."

Though Pastor Lewis continued the sermon, Emma heard very little of it. Her mind was focused on the initial words and how she could change her heart and mindset to put Jesus first in her life. Before she knew it, the service was over, and Jennie was tapping her arm.

"It's over," she said.

"Oh, so it is," Emma said. "Did you enjoy the message, William?"

"I did," he said, meeting her eyes. "I felt like he was speaking directly to me."

"That's funny," Emma said with a smile. "I felt the same way." The surrounding sounds seemed to diminish as he returned her smile. He had a nice smile though his lips were a little crooked. She wanted to reach out and touch them. Those thin, crooked lips.

"Can we go now?" Jennie whined. "I'm getting hungry."

"Of course," Emma said, shaking her head to clear the thought of William's lips away. "Let's go home and fill that empty tummy of yours." She tickled Jennie, earning a shrill giggle in return before the girl raced out of the pew ahead of them.

"Look, Emma, Pa's back." The young girl pointed toward the back of the church before sprinting off to hug her father.

Relief flooded Emma that her father was okay, followed quickly by a sadness. She glanced at William beside her. With her father back and William healing as quickly as he had, her father was sure to discharge him and then William would be on his way. Back to hunting outlaws and out of her life. She found she didn't want him to go. Though she believed she would never love another man the way she had loved Joseph, she could not deny there was some attraction building with William. She wanted him to stay, so she could learn more about him.

William's eyes met hers. Was she mistaken or was the same disappointment etched in his gaze? Could it be that he felt something for her as well? Emma hadn't felt anything for a man since Joseph's death and now she was developing feelings for the one man who wouldn't stick around? Pastor Lewis's words echoed again in her head. God had a plan they couldn't always see.

"Well, it's nice to see you up and about," her father said as they reached him. "I assume Emma has taken good care of you."

"Indeed she has," William said, shooting a look Emma's direction that heated her cheeks again.

"Oh, except I haven't changed the dressing today," Emma said, her hand flying to her mouth. William appeared to be recovering so well, she had almost forgotten it needed to be done. "I can do it as soon as we get home."

"No need," her father said, waving his hand. "I'll do a quick examination after lunch just to make sure everything is healing as it should be, and I can change the bandage then," her father said.

A strange surge of disappointment filled Emma, and she realized she had enjoyed changing his bandage as it gave her a reason to be close and touch him. What was wrong with her? Why hadn't she guarded her heart better?

"That will be fine," William said with a nod, and he and Emma followed the rest of their family outside and back to the house.

While her father examined William, Emma helped Carrie with the roast and vegetables for lunch.

"Will you pay attention?" Carrie said, taking the knife from Emma. "You very nearly cut off your finger. What's wrong with you?"

"Do you think he'll leave right away?" Emma asked.

"What are you talking about?" Carrie asked as she finished chopping up the potatoes. "Pa just got back. Why would he leave again right away?"

"Not Pa," Emma said with a sigh.

Carrie stopped chopping and stared at her. Her eyes grew round as she understood Emma's hint. "Oh, William? Why? Are you developing feelings for him?"

"I don't know," Emma said frustrated. "I've only

known the man for three days, so I shouldn't be developing feelings for him, right?"

"You had only known Joseph for a week when you were sure he was the one," Carrie pointed out as she dropped the vegetables in the boiling water.

Emma thought back and realized Carrie was right. "But William is different. He's not the type to stay in one place."

"Have you asked him?" Carrie asked pointing the wooden spoon in her hand at Emma. "Maybe he took the bounty hunter job because he had nothing keeping him in one place and maybe he would stay if he had something or *someone* worth staying for."

Emma bit her lip as she thought about Carrie's words. Could her sister be right? Could William stay in one place and be happy? Did she even have anything to offer him?

CHAPTER THIRTEEN

D oc Moore stepped back and rubbed his chin. "Well, your wound is healing and doesn't appear infected, but I'm still a little worried there might be fragments in your neck. If there are any, a jarring impact could cause them to shift and puncture your trachea - your windpipe."

"What are you saying?" William asked. Though still a little stiff, the pain had lessened each day, but a part of him hoped the doctor would tell him he needed more rest with supervision. He didn't know why, but Emma had wormed her way into his thoughts. There was a definite attraction between them and William half hoped to see where it might lead, but collecting bounties was his life. Could he give it up and stay in one place? Would she even want what little he had to offer?

"I'm saying you're free to go, but you should be careful. Chasing outlaws may not be the safest occupation for your condition."

No, stopping hunting outlaws wasn't likely in his future. There was too much adrenaline with it, and of course the money was nice. He didn't know what he had been thinking. He couldn't stay, but he did have one thing he wanted to do before he left. "Would it be possible to stay one more night with you? I can't get Monroe out of jail until tomorrow. I'd be happy to sleep on the couch."

"Nonsense," Doc Moore said. "You are welcome to stay another night. I'll bunk with the boys tonight.

"Thank you, sir. You have been too kind." William wondered if Doc Moore would be so accommodating if he knew of William's involvement in Joseph's death.

"It is I who should be thanking you. You keep the riff-raff out of our towns, which keeps everyone safe."

William averted his eyes as he thought again of Emma's husband. He hadn't kept everyone safe, but he had to find a way to tell Emma the truth.

"It smells like the girls have lunch ready, and I don't know about you, but I'm famished," Doc

Moore said, patting his belly. "The girls in Opdyke West could use some lessons from my daughters."

William smiled and followed him into the kitchen, but his mind was on Emma. Maybe he could get her to take a walk with him after lunch, and he could tell her everything then. He pulled out a chair and sat down, catching Emma's eye as he did. She smiled at him - a friendly, engaging, beautiful smile - and the guilt inside him grew.

With Doc Moore at the table, everyone's positions had shifted a little and Emma ended up next to him.

"Let's hold hands as we pray tonight," Doc Moore said.

William caught the flash of pink that graced Emma's fair cheeks before she held her hand out to him. He took her hand, but he couldn't enjoy the contact much as he was still thinking about how she might react to his information. Would she hate him? He certainly wouldn't blame her if she did. Would she never want to see him again? Would it matter? He was leaving, wasn't he?

"Amen," the family said.

William blinked as he glanced around. He had been so distracted he had missed the prayer? Emma looked at him with a quizzical expression but said nothing. William tried to stay more focused through the rest of lunch. The children took turns filling their father in on the days he had missed, and he in turn shared details of his time in Opdyke West.

When everyone was finally through eating, William caught Emma's hand as she passed by him. "Would you do me the honor of a walk? I'd like to finish that tour we started."

Emma glanced to her father for permission, and after a nod of his head, she stated her agreement, "It would be my pleasure to join you."

William tried to gather his thoughts as they stepped outside, but no matter how he formed the words in his head, he couldn't make them sound right.

"Did you have a particular place in mind you'd like to go?" Emma asked.

"No, let's just walk," he stated. Maybe the movement would help his brain, and he didn't think he could bear sitting while he said what needed to be said.

With a nod, she led the way toward the outer rim of town.

"I wanted to say thank you first of all for inviting me to church today. I think I heard some things I really needed to hear," he began.

"Oh, I'm so glad," she said. "Pastor Lewis has a knack for that, saying what people need to hear."

"Yes, I guess he does," William agreed. "I wanted to tell you why I was reluctant to attend at first." Though he hadn't originally planned on bringing up Catherine, he felt that perhaps if she knew of his own suffering she might understand his actions better.

She turned a curious eye his direction but said nothing and William inhaled deeply to gather the strength to continue. "I once was a committed believer like you. I was married to the woman I loved, working a job I enjoyed, and I believed in a God above who was looking out for me. Until the day I saw Catherine shot."

Emma gasped and clutched her hand to her mouth. "Oh, William."

"There was a fight occurring in the saloon and the men got carried away and drew their guns. The bartender pushed them outside but not before a few shots were fired. Catherine was leaving the mercantile and coming to meet me for lunch when the bullet hit her. I was a Deputy Sheriff at the time and the front window faced the street. I heard the gunshot, and I saw Catherine crumble. I rushed into the street, but there was nothing I could do. She died in my arms."

"William, I'm so sorry," Emma said, her eyes shiny with unshed tears.

William swallowed the lump of emotion welling up and cleared his throat a few times. "After Catherine, I grew angry with God. How could He love me and let my wife die? And especially like that? After Catherine's death, I joined the Texas Rangers before becoming a bounty hunter because I thought staying busy would keep me from missing Catherine."

Emma stopped, turned to him, and placed her hand on his arm. "I felt the same way when Joseph was taken, but God's plan is bigger than we know. If He loved us enough to send his son to die for us, then I have to trust He loves me even when things happen that I don't understand."

William smiled. "That's what your sister said this morning that convinced me to go."

"Jennie?" Emma asked with a laugh and then shook her head. "She is too bright for her own good sometimes."

"She is," William said, taking Emma's hand from his arm and holding it in his own, "but I'm glad she is. I needed to hear that message this morning to realize I hadn't really been living, I had just been running."

Emma's gaze locked with his and her lips parted as she said, "What do you need to be living again?"

William took a deep breath as he gazed into the emerald green of her gaze. Could he tell her? He didn't want the way she looked at him to change, and he feared once she knew the truth the affection he read now would disappear. Still, he couldn't NOT tell her, so with a final swallow, he gathered his courage and opened his mouth, "I need…."

"You have some nerve, Cook," a male voice broke the moment. William dropped Emma's hands and turned to see the man from the previous day staring him down. His hands were clenched at his side and a vein bulged on his forehead.

"Carl, William is our guest," Emma said, obviously shocked at his behavior.

Carl's brows shot up his forehead. "It's William, now is it? Do you even know who this man is, Emma?"

"I know he's a bounty hunter who was injured and needed our help. He's been nothing but nice to my family…"

"This is Wild Bill Cook," Carl said, letting the words resonate with her. "I asked around about you," he said, narrowing his eyes at William. "You thought you could hide what you'd done by changing your name, but I know who you are and what you did."

"I wasn't trying to hide anything," William began.

Beside him Emma gasped, halting the conversation between the two men. "You… you were the Ranger in charge of the Holden mission."

William's face paled and his shoulders dropped, but he didn't deny it. "I was."

"You were the reason my husband was killed," Emma said, her previous soft voice now dripping with anger. "Why didn't you tell me?"

"I didn't know at first," William said, shaking his head. "It wasn't until you mentioned Holden yesterday that I made the connection. I spent all day yesterday and today trying to think of the best way to tell you, but I couldn't find the right words."

"Or didn't want to," Carl said, a satisfied smirk on his face.

"Emma, I'm sorry. It's why I suggested this walk. I was going to tell you everything, I…" William reached out a hand to her, but Emma shook her head and backed away from him.

"You should have told me as soon as you knew." Her voice was low and accusatory. "I need time to think," she said, taking another step back. "Don't follow me." Her eyes held William's gaze before flicking to Carl. "Either of you." With that, she turned and rushed away from town.

"Did you honestly think she would fall for you?" Carl asked, turning to William.

Anger swirled through William's body. "You better get out of my sight before I pretend I got my mark wrong," he said, dropping his hand to his gun.

Carl narrowed his eyes as he looked from William's wound to the gun. "I've heard you are a strong shot, but do you think you could hit the mark with your wound?"

William narrowed his eyes and stared the man down. "I don't know. Do you want to find out?"

Carl opened his mouth as if he were going to say something more, then thought better of it and walked away.

William watched him go, his hands shaking against his thighs. He would never shoot a man in the back, but if that man had ruined his chance to tell Emma his side of the story…. No, he would not retaliate. That would make him no better than Carl. He'd find another way to reach Emma.

CHAPTER FOURTEEN

mma didn't stop walking until she found herself in the purple sage fields. How could she have been so stupid? She had fallen not only for a man who would never stay but for the very man responsible for her husband's death.

"Help me understand, God," she said aloud as she skimmed the sage bushes with her hand. "Why did you send him here and why did you bring him into my life? I know I don't know the whole story but help me understand at least that much."

The wind blew softly around her, rustling the purple leaves, but no answer came. The fields normally filled her with peace, but no peace came this time. With a sigh, Emma turned around and headed back to the homestead. Hopefully, William would have returned, grabbed his things, and left by the time she arrived.

"Where's William?" Carrie asked as Emma entered the house.

"You mean he hasn't already been here?" Emma asked, a mixture of hope and anger fighting for control within her. Maybe she should have listened to his explanation. Maybe he had been about to tell her the truth.

Carrie shook her head, her freckled face filled with questions.

Emma shook away the hope, letting the anger take over. No, he could have and should have told her under the tree when he first realized. This behavior just proved he was not trustworthy. "Well, I'm sure Mr. Cook will be here soon to grab his things. I doubt he will be staying much longer with us." With that, Emma turned on her heel and hurried into the shared bedroom, shutting the door behind her.

She curled up in the bed, thankful that Jennie wasn't in the room and let the tears flow down her cheeks. Why had God brought this man into her life? Why had He allowed the wound of pain to be refreshed? Would she ever have another chance at love like she had with Joseph?

As the tears fell down her cheeks, and she mumbled her questions to God, exhaustion descended upon her and her eyes closed.

CHAPTER FIFTEEN

W illiam had no idea how long he walked, but the sun was low in the sky when he returned to the homestead. He hoped Emma would have calmed down enough to hear him out, but he couldn't blame her reaction.

Carrie and Doc Moore met him at the front door. "What did you do to my sister?" Carrie asked, hands on her hips and fire shooting from her eyes. William admired her fierce loyalty but felt for the man who would marry her in the future as her gaze was penetrating and convicting.

"I didn't mean to," William said softly. "I was trying to find a way to tell her that I was the Ranger in charge of the operation that got Joseph killed, but I wasn't fast enough. Carl found out first and told her before I had a chance."

Carrie gasped, and her hand flew to her mouth. She narrowed her eyes at him and opened her mouth as if she were about to chastise him. Then her mouth closed and with a shake of her head, she spun on her heel and entered the house, letting the door slam behind her.

"I'll talk with her later," Doc Moore said staring at the closed door for a minute before turning his attention back to William. "So why don't you tell me the situation?" Doc Moore pointed to the stools that sat on the porch.

William sighed as he sat down. "I never thought I'd meet Joseph's widow or the other man's - there was another man killed in the excursion. I never even envisioned this kind of life for myself. I wanted to serve my town and protect the citizens, but when I lost my wife, Catherine, I lost myself as well. I joined the Rangers, which helped for a time, but then I was approached about becoming a hunter. The money called to me, and it was that first job where I recruited Rangers and Joseph answered the call.

"The round up went well until one of the men tried to escape. My team went after him and I thought we had him subdued, but then he managed to pull Joseph's weapon and shot him and two other men before my men knew what was happening.

"I should have been the one to deliver the news as I was the one in charge of the men, but I was no longer a Ranger. I began collecting bounties full time after that job. Maybe I was running, not only from Catherine's death but also from the other men, but then I landed here, and I met Emma."

"Yes, let's talk about Emma," Doc Moore said, folding his hands on his lap. He had been quiet during William's story, but William sensed he had issues on his mind. "What are your intentions toward my daughter?"

The question caught William off guard. He thought after his story that Doc Moore would be shooing him off the property, not asking what his intentions were with Emma. "To be honest, sir, I'm not sure. I hadn't planned on falling for anyone here, and I'm not sure I could give up hunting outlaws, but your daughter has made quite an impression on me. I find myself thinking of her often, and the guilt from not telling her the whole story ate me up for two days."

Doc Moore's brow arched, but he said nothing, letting William flounder through his feelings.

"I don't know that it matters now though. She ran

off without letting me explain. It's probably for the best that I'm leaving tomorrow."

"Perhaps it is," Doc Moore said leaning back, but William felt there was more to his words than he was letting on.

"If I need to, I can sleep in the barn with the horse tonight," William continued. "I don't want to upset Emma any more than I already have."

"Oh, I think Emma will be alright," Doc Moore said, "but I wouldn't be surprised if she stays in her room until she know's you're gone."

William nodded and followed Doc Moore's lead into the house. Carrie glared at him initially from the kitchen while she prepared dinner, but after a discussion with Doc Moore, her demeanor softened, and she appeared slightly less hostile toward him. William had no idea what the doctor had told her, but he welcomed the reprieve from her scolding eyes.

While he helped entertain the younger two with card tricks, his mind wandered to what he would say to Emma when she entered the room, but when supper was ready, and Emma still hadn't appeared, he began to accept the fact he might not see her again before leaving.

"Aren't we waiting for Emma?" Benjamin asked as they took their places around the table.

"Emma isn't feeling well tonight," Doc Moore said. "So, we are going to let her sleep and not bother her."

"Does that mean I can't sleep in the room tonight?" Jennie asked.

"We'll sleep in the living room tonight," Carrie said, patting her sister's arm. "You can take the couch and I'll take the chair."

"Okay," Jennie said with a shrug as she scooped up some beans and shoveled them into her mouth.

With the topic of Emma dropped, the rest of dinner was quiet. Before William knew it, the food was gone, and Carrie was picking up the plates to wash them.

"Do you really have to leave tomorrow?" Benjamin asked as they sat around the table after dinner.

"I do," William said, realizing it wasn't just Emma he would miss, but the rest of her family as well. "I have to return a bad man to the authorities."

"Will you come back after that?" Benjamin hounded.

"I don't know," William answered truthfully. "My life isn't here. My life is out hunting men who break the law."

"But what about Emma?" Jennie asked, her innocent eyes large and round.

"Emma will be fine without me," William said, though he was beginning to wonder if he'd be fine without Emma. "In fact, she'll probably be better off without me."

"I doubt that," Carrie spoke up softly as she picked up the last plate from the table.

William could have asked her what she meant by that, but it didn't matter. He'd be leaving in the morning and Emma would be only a memory, which was where she belonged.

CHAPTER SIXTEEN

William woke before the sun. Not that he had slept much anyway. He had stayed up hoping Emma would enter the living room, so he could talk to her. When that didn't happen, and it became clear the girls wanted to go to sleep, he had retired to the room, but with one ear attuned to the noises in the living room, what little sleep he had received had been restless.

With a sigh, William pushed back the blanket and sat up. The pain still throbbed with excessive movement, but it had softened to a dull, manageable ache. He gave it a moment to recede before standing and crossing to his saddlebag.

After pulling on his clothes, William folded up the few items he had unpacked and shoved them back in the saddlebag. He spared a final glance around the room to make sure he hadn't missed anything before heading to the kitchen.

He didn't expect anyone else was awake, but he was hopeful he could locate the coffee and brew a pot before having to head out. However, he was pleasantly surprised to find Doc Moore reading at the table, Carrie already bustling in the kitchen, and a pot of coffee already made.

"Good morning, Mr. Cook," Doc Moore said, looking up from his Bible as William entered. "Would you like some eggs before you leave?"

"If it isn't too much trouble," William said, being careful to keep his voice low as Jennie was still asleep on the couch.

"It's no trouble," Carrie said. "There's coffee made too. Go on and help yourself."

William nodded and grabbed a cup off the shelf, feeling very much at home and like an outsider at the same time. He filled the mug, added a dash of milk, and returned to the table with the warm liquid in hand.

As he sat down, Carrie placed a plate of eggs, bacon, and a slice of bread in front of him. "Thank you," he said, smiling up at her before picking up his fork.

"Aren't you going to pray first?" Doc Moore asked.

William dropped his gaze. "It's been quite a while since I prayed. I'm not sure I remember how."

"Then I'll pray for you," the doctor said and closed his eyes. "Lord, we thank you for this food and for the hands that prepared it. Thank you for healing William. Keep him safe on his journey and help him find his way back to you. Amen."

"Amen," William echoed though he felt strange listening to someone else pray for him.

He ate his breakfast in silence, unsure how to bring up the topic of Emma. Doc Moore had made it pretty clear the previous night that Emma may want nothing more to do with him and that he might not see her before leaving, but he felt he at least owed her an apology.

"Do you have any paper and a pen?" William asked when his plate was clean, and his belly was full.

Doc Moore nodded, walked to a small chest in the living room, and returned a moment later with a few sheets of paper and a pen.

William stared at the blank page for a minute wondering how to write what was in his head. After a deep breath, he placed the pen on the sheet and let the words flow. When he was finished, he folded the letter and wrote Emma's name on the outside.

"Will you make sure she gets this?" William asked Carrie as he stood.

"Of course. I'll put it in our room where she'll be sure to find it," Carrie said. As she took the paper from him, she flashed him a small sympathetic smile.

"Alright, I guess I should be going then," William said. "Can you show me where my horse is lodged?"

"Be happy to," Doc Moore said, standing and leading the way outside.

The air was crisp and cool as they walked to the barn, and the first rays of sunlight were hitting the sky, creating a brilliant purple and red color.

Doc Moore opened the barn door and crossed to the third stall. William was glad to see his horse munching hay happily in the stall. She looked well taken care of.

He entered the stall and let Bessie sniff his hand. She had been his first purchase when he joined the Rangers and she had been his closest friend since.

"Thank you again for boarding her and taking care of her while I recovered," William said, pulling out a small wad of bills and handing it over to Doc Moore.

The doctor shook his head, but William insisted,

"You fed me, so consider it repayment for food. Besides, I make more than enough money for myself."

With a single nod, the doctor accepted the money and shoved it in his pocket. "You're welcome, Mr. Cook. Now, if you don't mind, I need to throw my two cents in. I can tell by the way you look at my daughter that you have feelings for her and the very action of her shutting herself in her room proves she cares for you as well. I know you must turn your bounty in, but there comes a time in a man's life when he realizes the chase is no longer what it once was. There is a comfort in coming home to a loyal woman.

"I know you had that once," Doc Moore continued when William opened his mouth to speak. "And I know you say you don't want it again, but iffen you ever do, I'd be willing to get to know you better."

"Thank you, Sir," William said, unsure of what else to say. That very thought had been playing in his head like a record since the day before. How nice it had been to come home to a loving woman and how it could be that way again if he could give up bounty hunting. But therein lay the quandary. Could he give up the life?

The doctor said nothing further as he helped William saddle Bessie up.

"Be sure to keep your wound clean and covered for another week or so," he said as William mounted Bessie outside the barn. "And be seen by a doctor if you have any issues breathing or the pain gets worse."

"I will, thank you," William said. He spared one final look at the man who had saved his life and then glanced at the house in hopes of at least seeing Emma in the window. Nothing but empty windows greeted him back and with a sigh, William turned the horse towards town. He had a bounty to collect and a woman to forget.

CHAPTER SEVENTEEN

The house was quiet when Emma woke the next morning. She looked to the side, but the bed was empty. Where was everyone? Pa would most likely be at work and Jennie and Benjamin would be at school, but where were Carrie and Samuel? Emma was just surprised they had let her sleep in. Of course, usually she was awoken by Jennie first thing in the morning.

After a quick stretch, Emma rolled out of bed and dressed for the day. Her calico dress was nothing fancy, but it was one of her favorites as evidenced by the fraying hem at the bottom.

She opened the bedroom door, expecting to hear Carrie cleaning in the kitchen or see her sitting in the living room, sewing, but there was nothing but silence.

"Hello?" Emma called as she walked toward the kitchen. The dishes were washed and drying by the sink save for a plate with a few pancakes on it, obviously saved for her. A wave of hunger knotted her stomach as she realized she had missed dinner the previous night in her effort to avoid William.

Grabbing the plate, she sat down at the table and that's when she saw the note. Her name was at the top, written in her sister's handwriting.

Emma,

William is gone. I do think you should have listened to his story for Joseph's death wasn't really his fault. We decided to let you sleep as it seemed you needed it, so to make sure it was quiet for you, I decided to help Pa out in the clinic today. Samuel is working the garden should you need anything. I pray you find peace and we'll see you this evening.

Carrie

Emma frowned at the paper as she cut the pancake into pieces and brought a forkful to her mouth. Had she been wrong not to listen to William? It wouldn't be the first time her emotions got the better of her, but usually she had a way to make it right. If William were gone though, there was no way to make it right, but maybe it was better this way. After all, even without the lying incident, he wouldn't have stayed, and Emma would still be alone, wouldn't she?

She pondered that question as she finished eating the pancakes. When she was finished, she washed her dishes and then looked around the room for what else she could do. Carrie was such a good homemaker that items were rarely out of place.

Emma wandered into the living room, but everything was put away here as well. She would venture into her father's and brothers' room, but they had often said they would rather she didn't, so she wandered back into the girls' room to grab some knitting.

As she reached for the knitting bucket beside the dresser, another flash of white caught her eye. It was another note, but this one wasn't written in her sister's curly script. Instead, her name was spelled out in a crooked print.

Intrigued, Emma grabbed the note and sat down on the bed to read it.

Dear Emma,

I hope Carrie left this for you. I'm sorry things ended so poorly between us, and I wish I could go back and tell you the moment I knew, but I was scared. I haven't felt affection for a woman since Catherine, but I was feeling attraction to you, and

I was afraid you would be angry when you found out. I don't know if you felt the same way I did, nor do I know if I could have offered you the kind of life you want. Perhaps it worked out this way for a reason, but I wanted to thank you for caring for my injury and to let you know how sorry I was. If I could go back in time and make sure Gilbert was truly secured and bring Joseph back to you, I would.

William Cook

Emma fought the emotion as she read the letter again and pored over each word. Had she acted too hastily? It didn't matter now, of course. William was gone, and she had no way to reach him. The enormity of that hit her and the letter fell from her hands as she curled into a ball and let the tears come once more.

CHAPTER EIGHTEEN

"What took so long?" Jack Hardesty asked as William deposited Monroe in his care. "This was supposed to be a quick and easy hunt."

"I took a bullet," William growled. "I had to take a few days to heal. I was lucky it hit a fleshy part and didn't cause other damage."

He had been grumpy all day since picking Monroe up from the Sage Creek jail. William had thought once he left the town that the image of Emma would fade from his mind and he would remember the thrill of collecting bounties, but Monroe had been nothing but a hassle since they left.

William had bound his hands to the front of the saddle and then, after getting Monroe mounted on the horse, had tied his feet to the saddle belt to keep him from kicking. Monroe had fought but not as much as William had expected. Instead, he had pleaded his case the entire ride. William grew so tired of his voice that he almost knocked the man out.

"I have another mark," Jack said. "You think you can handle it or should I give it to someone else."

"I can take it," William said. Whether he could or not he needed to. He needed to stay busy to keep his mind and his heart from wandering to the blond woman he had left behind.

"Good," Jack said. "Well, here's the cut for Monroe and the next mark." He slid a plump white envelope and a folded piece of paper across the desk.

William picked up the envelope first and glanced inside to see it bursting with bills. Then he unfolded the piece of paper. A grim looking man with a long thin face stared back at him.

William scanned the paper. Tom "Too Tall" Herman wanted for bank robbery. Last seen near Dallas Texas. It was perfect. Far enough away to put distance between Emma and himself and with a paycheck of a thousand dollars, it was a nice job that should be challenging enough to keep him on his toes and his mind off a certain woman.

"Looks good. I'll head out now."

Jack nodded and turned his attention to Monroe.

After a quick stop at the mercantile to load up and replenish items he needed, William repacked his saddle bag, mounted Bessie, and headed toward Dallas. If he was lucky, he might make it by nightfall but more than likely, he'd be sleeping under the stars.

CHAPTER NINETEEN

W hen her tears were spent, Emma wandered back into the kitchen. She still had a few hours before the young ones would be out of school and a few more hours until her father and Carrie would be home. Samuel would probably finish his work around the small farm shortly after the young ones returned home.

Emma decided to spend the time cooking for supper. She began chopping vegetables for the stew, hoping to keep her mind off William Cook's strong face and cleft chin.

When the vegetables were ready, she added them and the meat to a large pot and lit the fire. As the stew began to simmer, she turned her attention to the bread. After the ingredients were mixed, she began kneading the dough, letting her mind flirt with "what if" possibilities.

If she had heard William out, would he have stayed? Beyond that, if he had stayed, would he have wanted to court her? Might she have one day been preparing bread for him in their house as she waited for him to come home for dinner?

"Mmm, what smells so good?"

Jennie's voice broke Emma's daydream, and she looked up to realize nearly an hour had passed and she hadn't gotten the bread in the stove yet. Benjamin and Jennie stood a few feet away staring at her.

"It's stew," Emma said, placing the bread in the stove, "but it's not ready yet. We're going to wait for Pa and Carrie to finish their day before we eat."

"Okay," Jennie said, a small pout gracing her lips. "Do you think William will ever come back?"

"Yeah, I miss him too," Benjamin said. "I wanted him to teach me about bounty hunting."

"Oh, I'm sorry you two, but I don't think Mr. Cook is coming back," Emma said.

"Emma, are you sad that William is gone?" Jennie asked.

Emma sighed. "I suppose I am a little, but Mr. Cook had to get back to his life. He would never have been happy staying here. Sage Creek doesn't have enough to offer him."

"It has us," Jennie said with a pout. She folded her arms across her chest. "I wanted him to stay. I wanted the two of you to get married so he could be with us always."

"Why are you so eager to marry me off?" Emma asked with a smile. "Won't you miss me when I don't live here any longer?"

"Yes," Jennie said, "but you seemed happier when you were married to Joseph."

Emma stared at the sage little girl. Of course she had been happier when she was married to Joseph, but that had been about Joseph and not just about marriage, right? Suddenly, she was no longer sure.

CHAPTER TWENTY

William made it to Dallas just as the sun was setting. At least he'd be able to sleep in a room tonight and ask some questions around town. If he was really lucky, maybe he'd even find his mark hanging around at the saloon though from his experience, bank robbers tended to be less social.

The inn's sign came into view and William dismounted, throwing the reins around the hitching post before sauntering into the three-story building.

The smell of leather greeted him as he stepped into the lobby. Two brown leather couches complemented the cream and brown colors of the room. A woman sat behind a check-in desk to the right.

She looked up as William approached and he

paused. With her blond hair and hazel eyes, she reminded him very much of Emma. He shook his head to clear the image - how had she affected him so profoundly after only a few days - and continued toward the woman. She wasn't Emma; he knew that. Emma was back in Sage Creek.

"Can I help you?" she asked.

"Yes, ma'am. I wanted to see if you have a room for a few nights."

She smiled at him as she opened a large book. "You might be in luck." After a quick scanning, she turned around and grabbed a key off the hook. "I have room three available."

"Wonderful." William plunked down the required bills and took the key. He would check the room out and stash his money before heading to the saloon to gather information. It was never smart to carry a lot of money into those places. You never knew when fights might break out or pickpockets would wander through.

A quick investigation of the room satisfied him, and after stashing the money under the bed, William locked the door behind him and headed toward the saloon.

The place was bustling when he arrived, not

unusual as these types of establishments catered to a night crowd.

He walked up to the bar and ordered his usual single shot of whiskey. The bartender had just slid the glass his direction when a heated argument broke out next to him.

"I told you to stay away from my sister, Charles." The words were slurred and angry.

"Your sister is old enough to make up her own mind, Leroy," the other man shot back, his voice much harder to understand. Both men had clearly had too much to drink.

William, wanting to distance himself from any fight so as not to draw attention, grabbed his drink and stood, but the men were quicker than he had expected and before he had fully turned, a fist appeared out of nowhere and connected with his neck.

The room grew grey as William grabbed his neck and sank to the floor. Hot, searing pain erupted in the wound and clawed up his neck. While the men brawled near him, he tried in vain to grab the attention of anyone close by, but everyone's gaze remained fixated on the two men and William lost his fight with the darkness.

CHAPTER TWENTY-ONE

"Thank you for finally coming out with me," Carl said, grabbing Emma's hand.

She fought the urge to extricate her hand from his grip as they walked. What had she been thinking? Giving Carl hope wasn't fair to either of them and she didn't need to be married to be happy. Emma had accepted the invitation to the town picnic in a moment of weakness and now she was regretting it.

"You're welcome, but Carl, I hope you understand this doesn't mean we are courting. This is just two friends attending a town social event together."

"Don't be silly, Emma," he said. "You know we belong together, and after this afternoon, I'm sure you'll remember how much fun we used to have."

Emma swallowed her sigh. This was going to be a long few hours.

The church grounds were already littered with blankets and townspeople when they arrived. Carl found an open patch and spread out a blanket for them. Emma set the picnic basket she had packed down and then folded her feet under her.

"Would you like some punch?" Carl asked.

"That would be nice," Emma said.

He returned a few minutes later with a cup of lemonade for them both. After handing her a cup, he sat as well, placing himself a little too close to Emma for her comfort.

"Are you hungry?" she asked, shifting her position to discreetly put more space between them. She opened the picnic basket. "I have cheese, biscuits, and fruit."

"Do you remember the first barn dance we attended?" he asked, ignoring her question and scooting closer again.

Emma knew he was referring to the dance where they had cuddled in the haystack before being found by Samuel. She had thought then she was going to marry Carl, not necessarily because she loved him, but because he was nice to her and they got along. The concept wasn't romantic but practical marriages were the way of the west and in a practical concept, they had made sense.

"Yes, Carl, I remember, but that was a long time ago." Emma pulled out the cheese and fruit and placed it on a plate in front of them.

"It doesn't have to be," he said, leaning toward her. "We could share those feelings again."

"I'm sorry, Carl. This was a mistake," Emma said, dropping the piece of cheese she had picked up and standing. "I thought we could revisit being friends, but it appears we have two different views of our relationship."

"Emma, wait," Carl said, pushing himself up and reaching out to her.

"No, Carl, I need time to think. I'll see you later." Before he could protest any further, Emma spun around and hurried home.

CHAPTER TWENTY-TWO

When William awoke, his throat felt funny. Stiff and sore but also cold. The cot he was on was stiff, though covered in a sheet, and the room felt sterile. A hospital? The memory of the bar fight flooded back. He was beginning to have very bad luck in saloons.

William raised his hand to touch his neck but before his hand reached the skin, a woman entered the room.

"Don't touch," she scolded. "It hasn't had time to heal yet."

William opened his mouth to speak but his vocal chords did not seem to be working.

"You can't speak," the woman said, coming

closer. "Due to some bullet fragments shifting in your neck, your windpipe closed. The doctor was forced to perform a tracheotomy."

William's eyes grew round. Though not sure exactly what that meant, it didn't sound good.

"He was able to retrieve all the fragments, and your neck should heal soon so we can remove the tube. The procedure heals quickly after that, but you'll have to be careful to avoid injuring your neck in the future."

The door opened again, and a man entered. "Oh, good, you're awake. Has Nurse Johnson informed you of your condition?"

William nodded, knowing trying to speak would be useless.

"Good, let me check the tube to see if we can take it out yet."

As the doctor came closer, William wondered how long he had been out. Would his mark even still be in town or would he be long gone by now? Did he even still care? If his neck wound did require him to stop bounty hunting, it would be the perfect excuse to retire and he couldn't think of any place he'd rather do that than Sage Creek.

"Alright, the wound is healing nicely. I'm going to

remove the tube and we'll let the wound close. You'll probably need to stay while it's healing but once it's closed over, you should be free to go."

William nodded and closed his eyes as the doctor prepared for the procedure.

CHAPTER TWENTY-THREE

"How long are you going to hide from him?" Carrie asked Emma as they rolled out dough to make cookies. It was Saturday afternoon, a time when the girls tried to bake and talk, though usually Jennie was scurrying around their feet as they did. Today, she had gone with Pa and the boys into town to pick up a few things.

"I don't know what you're talking about," Emma said, averting her gaze and pretending to focus on the rolling pin.

"Yes, you do. It's been nearly a week since you went to the picnic with Carl and you've barely left the house since."

Emma sighed. "He was a great friend once, but

now he's obsessed with marrying me, and I just can't do it."

"Because of William?" Carrie teased with a knowing smile.

"It's stupid, right?" Emma asked. "I ran him off by not listening to him and now I can't stop thinking about him. I tell myself it would never work, but I can't deny the attraction was there. Maybe not quite the same as Joseph, but close, and I never thought I would find that again."

A look of sympathy covered Carrie's face. "Maybe he'll come back," she offered half-heartedly. "I know he cared about you."

Emma shook her head and rolled her eyes. "No, my impetuousness has finally caught up to me. I need to get used to the fact that he's really gone and move on, but I can't marry Carl just to marry someone. I'll just have to hope that God forgives my wasting this opportunity and grants me another."

Before Carrie could reply, a knock sounded at the front door. The girls shared a look of confusion and trepidation. With the rest of the family in town, it was only the two of them in the house. While patients did come to the house on occasion, it didn't happen often.

"I'll get the rifle," Emma said. "Why don't you go hide in our room?"

Though fear shone in Carrie's green eyes, she shook her head resolutely. "No, if you're going to answer the door then I'm coming too."

"Alright," Emma nodded, leading the way to the front door where the rifle was kept. The rapping came again as she grabbed the gun and checked to make sure it was loaded.

"Carrie, on my count, open the door," Emma said, bracing the gun against her shoulder as Samuel had taught her. "Now."

Carrie swung the door open and towards her, using it almost like a shield between her and the person on the other side.

"William?" Emma's voice was breathless with disbelief and she blinked her eyes a few times to make sure she wasn't dreaming.

"Hi, Emma," he said as a crooked smile graced his lips. "Thanks for not shooting me, but are you going to make me stand out here all day or are you going to invite me in?" His voice sounded different, a little scratchier and the bandage around his neck didn't look like the ones her father used, but it was William all the same.

Still not trusting her eyes, Emma eased the

hammer back down and nodded. "Of course, come in." She lowered the gun and leaned it against the wall.

"Hi, Carrie," William said as he stepped over the threshold and closed the door behind him. A moment of awkward silence fell as the girls looked at William and waited for an explanation. He cleared his throat and shoved his hands in his pockets.

If Emma hadn't known better, she would have sworn William was nervous, but she had never seen him nervous. Did bounty hunters even feel nervous?

CHAPTER TWENTY-FOUR

W illiam stared at his boots as he gathered his courage. Emma hadn't kicked him out already so that was a good sign. Maybe Carrie or one of the other family members had told her his side of the story. Still, just because she was being civil didn't mean she felt as he did and that was the scary part.

What if he had ridden all the way out here to confess his feelings only to find out she was no longer interested? What would he do then?

"I suppose you're wondering why I'm here," he said slowly as he raised his eyes to meet Emma's.

"The thought had crossed my mind," she said with a smile.

That smile bolstered his courage and William

took a step her direction. "I came back for you, Emma. I know we didn't leave on good terms, and I thought I could forget you, but the whole time I was bringing Monroe in, you were all I could think of. I don't know how you got in my head, Emma Stewart, but I can't seem to get you out."

"Oh," Carrie sighed, grabbing both Emma's and William's attention. "That's so romantic."

"Out," Emma said to Carrie, pointing to the kitchen before grabbing William's arm and leading him into the living room. She sat on the couch and motioned for him to sit beside her which William did willingly. He longed to reach out and take her hand, but he restrained himself.

"I can't believe you came back." Her eyes were focused on her lap, and her voice was barely more than a whisper. "I thought I was justified in my anger at you, but even before Carrie told me the whole story, I began to regret pushing you away. Of course by the time I swallowed my pride, you were already gone." Her eyes flicked up to his. "I honestly never thought I'd see you again."

It was the invitation he needed. He could see her heart in her jade eyes and he reached for her hand, enjoying the delicate feel of her skin against his.

"I wasn't sure I would ever see you again either,"

he said, "but as I lay in the hospital bed healing this week, I found that I didn't care about the money or the adrenaline any longer. I only cared about you."

Emma's eyes widened, and her gaze shifted to the bandage around his neck. "Did you re-injure it?"

His lips pulled into a tight smile. He had to tell her, but he hoped the truth wouldn't scare her away. "I didn't get out of the way fast enough when a fight broke out in a saloon. The punch shifted some bullet fragments and cut off my air supply. They were forced to do a tracheotomy until I could breathe again, but they think they got all the pieces this time. I'll always have a scar, Emma, and I don't know that there won't be complications later. I know I'm not offering you much, but I'm offering you all I have."

Tears shimmered in Emma's eyes as she shook her head. "You stupid man. I don't care about a scar or complications. My father is a doctor, remember? I'm just glad you're okay."

William wiped a tear from her eye and left his hand on her cheek. She sighed and leaned against it for a moment before jerking up.

"I can't leave Sage Creek though, William. I'm not the kind of woman who would enjoy the life of a bounty hunter."

"I guess it's a good thing I gave it up then," he

said with a smile and then, even though he knew he probably shouldn't, William leaned forward and touched Emma's lips with his own. It was only a moment, but it was enough to solidify any lingering doubts he had. This woman was his future.

CHAPTER TWENTY-FIVE

Emma ran the brush through her long blond hair one last time as she regarded her image in the mirror.

"If you don't stop brushing it, it may all fall out," Carrie teased from across the room.

"Can that happen?" Jennie asked with wide eyes.

"No, of course not," Emma answered with a laugh. "Carrie is just teasing me."

"I wouldn't have to if you would stop preening in front of that mirror. You look lovely."

Emma glanced down at her dark green velvet dress. The neckline was wide and showed off her slender shoulders and the color complemented her eyes. It wasn't a new dress, but it was one William hadn't seen yet, and she hoped he would enjoy it.

"I just want it to be perfect," Emma said, running her hand down the dress to smooth out any wrinkles. "It's our first dance together."

"And it won't be the last," Carrie said crossing to the mirror and checking her own reflection. "I bet William proposes to you any day now."

Emma couldn't help but smile at the thought. The signs were all pointing that direction. He had begun building a homestead near her father's house as she had told him this side of town was her favorite. At this point, he didn't have to work as he had saved most of his money from his bounties and had plenty to finish the house and live comfortably until he decided what he wanted to do next.

"I hope so," Emma said. "I'm so glad Pa and everyone appears to have accepted him into the fold again."

"Well, everyone except Carl," Carrie joked.

Emma's face fell as she thought of Carl. He was the one hitch in her happiness. Ever since William had returned, and they had begun attending town functions together, Carl had become stoic and reclusive. Emma hadn't wanted to hurt him, and she truly hoped he would find a woman who could truly appreciate him soon, but she also had to do what was right for her.

"Can we go now?" Jennie asked, breaking the somber mood that had fallen on Emma.

"Yes, Jennie Bean, let's get out of here," Emma said, taking the little girl's hand and pulling her out of the room.

CHAPTER TWENTY-SIX

William sucked in his breath as Emma entered the living room. Her eyes sparkled as she smiled at Jennie beside her, and the green of her dress was breathtaking. He couldn't believe she was actually his.

"You look beautiful," he said as he took a step toward her.

"Why thank you, William," she said and flashed him her special flirtatious smile.

The rest of the family filed into the room, and after checking to make sure all needed items were accounted for, they exited the house and began the short walk to the barn.

Lighted lanterns hung from the open doors creating a soft romantic glow. William couldn't have been happier. This would be the perfect setting for the question he wanted to ask Emma.

As soon as they were inside, Jennie and Benjamin raced to the back to begin sampling the food. Doc Moore wandered over to some of the other men and Samuel and Carrie split off to find their friends.

"Shall we dance?" William asked as he led Emma toward the dance floor.

"I'd love nothing more," she answered.

As his arms circled her, William thought again how perfect a fit she was in them. He had never expected to fall in love with another woman after Catherine, but as he twirled the beautiful blond woman around, he knew he had done just that. Yet he wasn't scared. In fact, he was exhilarated. The thought of a life with her filled him with excitement each day.

"You're not a bad dancer," Emma teased up at him.

"I'm actually a very good dancer," he responded. "It just takes me a minute to warm up."

"By the end of the night, I expect to be amazed then."

He tightened his grip on her and pulled her closer. "I'm amazed every day I spend with you," he whispered down at her.

A rosy pink color flooded her cheeks, and she shook her head. "Flattery will get you nowhere Mr. Cook."

"Well, then how about this?" Though the music played on, he stopped moving and dropped to one knee. "Emma Stewart, you have reopened my heart to God and to love and for that I am truly thankful. Will you do me the honor of being my wife?"

A silence fell as the crowd around them realized what was happening. Even the music stopped. Emma glanced around before returning her gaze to him. "Of course I'll marry you, William."

Clapping and cheers erupted around them, but William barely heard them. He stood, scooping the woman he loved up and twirled her around. Though he had not thought it possible, he had finally found his way home.

THE END!

P.S. If you want to know what happens with Carl, stay tuned for the Sage Creek Saga books coming soon and keep an eye out for William's and Emma's wedding story!

IT'S NOT QUITE THE END!

Did you enjoy — Lawfully Justified? If you did, please leave a review. It really helps. http://books2read.com/LJ

You won't want to miss the other ones in the series!

Turn the page for a sneak peek!

27

AUTHOR'S NOTE

First off, let me say how glad I am that you read this book. Lawfully Justified was my second historical romance, and while it was fun, it was also a lot of work researching. The train robbery was based on an actual story I read. Now, I have been away for awhile, but I have plans to return to Sage Creek.

So if you've enjoyed reading this author's note so far (and really, how could you not?) I am offering, for today only, a page where you can sign up for my weekly newsletter for the low, low price of absolutely nothing.

Included in this weekly newsletter are many wonderful things like pictures of my adorable children, chances to win awesome prizes, new releases and sales I might be holding, great books from other authors, and anything else that strikes my fancy and that I think you would enjoy.

Even better, I solemnly swear to only send out one newsletter a week (usually on Tuesday unless life gets in the way which with three kids it usually does). I will not spam you, sell your email address to solicitors or anyone else, or any of those other terrible things.

Join me here and receive a free novella as my thank-you gift for choosing to hang out with me. It's fun and entertaining. I promise.

Prayers and blessings,

Lorana

28

NOT READY TO SAY GOODBYE YET?

William and Emma were such fun to write that I didn't want to let them go, so I gave them a second story. Don't worry, I know Emma has some siblings that need their own story too. I will get there. I promise, but first let's take a look at their wedding story.

The Scarlet Wedding

HE WAS ready to get married...

Until an outlaw from his past comes back into his life. Now, he must put his wedding on hold to save the sister he hasn't see in years.

She can't believe he kept information from her...

Emma is shocked to learn that William has a sister and that he's leaving. What if he doesn't come back like her first husband?

A case of Scarlet Fever....

With everything else going wrong, Emma isn't

sure she can handle anymore. And then her sister gets sick. Is it Scarlet Fever?

Read on for a taste of The Scarlet Wedding....

29

THE SCARLET WEDDING PREVIEW

Summer 1883, Sage Creek, Texas

"You're so lucky," Carrie sighed brushing her long blond hair as the girls got ready for bed that night. "That proposal was so romantic."

"I'm sure yours will come soon." Emma smiled at her younger sister as she took her own hair down. "I saw you dancing with Phillip Alder, and he had stars in his eyes."

"What about me?" Jennie asked.

Emma laughed and tousled her youngest sister's brown hair. "You have a few years yet, Jennie Bean, but there's a man out there for you as well. You just have to be patient."

Jennie's lower lip fell out in an adorable pout. "I want to be older now. I want to be kissed like you were, Emma. It looked so romantic." She put her little hand on her forehead and fell onto the bed.

"Oh, dear. We have our work cut out for us with this one." Emma slipped her dress off and her nightgown on and climbed into bed beside six-year-old Jennie. Carrie followed suit and climbed in on the other side of Jennie.

"Have you thought about the wedding yet?" Carrie asked.

"He only proposed tonight." Emma's tone was dismissive as if she had thought of no such thing. The truth was she had already been thinking about the wedding. She wanted it in the church of course. Carrie would be a bridesmaid and Jennie the flower girl. Emma wondered if William would ask Samuel, her brother, to be his best man. The two had been spending a lot of time together building William's homestead, but there was also Jesse Jennings, who William had become close with.

Emma had also become good friends with Kate Jennings. The two were close in age and became friends when William began courting Emma. Once to twice a week, they would get together and trade secrets and recipes. They also spoke often of their desire to have children.

Kate would reach that milestone first. She was already with child and nearing her fifth month. Though Emma enjoyed seeing her friend grow, she couldn't help feeling jealous, and so she hoped William would be okay with a fairly short engagement. She wanted to start a family with him.

"I know he just proposed tonight," Carrie continued, "but I bet you've been thinking about the wedding since the first day he kissed you."

Emma was glad the light from the lantern was low so her sisters wouldn't see her blush. She had been thinking about the wedding since that day. Well, not the wedding itself, but the marriage.

She had already had one wedding, having been married to Joseph Stewart before a Texas Ranger mission cut his life short. So, even though weddings were enjoyable and beautiful, that wasn't her focus. Her focus was on being a wife and mother. Something she had hoped for with her first marriage, but it had ended so quickly it was almost nonexistent.

As much as Emma loved her family, she wanted to be a wife again, to run her own homestead, cook for her husband, and enjoy quiet times in front of the fire. And, eventually she hoped to fill the house with children, but that was at least a year away.

"Get some sleep," Emma said in answer. "We can talk more about the wedding tomorrow."

"Do I get to throw the flowers again?" Jennie's voice was heavy with sleep.

"Yes, Jennie Bean, you can throw the flowers. Now, go to sleep."

Carrie and Jennie obliged and soon were breathing softly beside her, but it was Emma's own mind that refused to shut down. When it wasn't reliving the wonderful night and the proposal, it was thinking forward to what had to be done for a wedding. She would need to make the cake, get flowers, and see if she could alter her old wedding dress a little. Emma couldn't afford a new one, and it would have been a frivolous waste of money anyway.

WILLIAM LEFT Emma's house after walking the girls home with a smile on his lips. Though he had been nearly certain she would say yes, there was always the small chance of a negative reply.

However, with the positive response, he could now relax and focus all his energy on finishing the homestead. It was nearly complete as he had spent the last few months on it, but he needed to finish daubing and acquire the rest of the furniture.

That would require a trip into a larger town though. Sage Creek was growing, and he could get tables and chairs there, but he wanted at least one special piece for Emma. Perhaps he could do that in the next few days.

"You're a hard man to track down."

William stiffened at the sound of the voice and reached for his gun. Retired or not, he still liked having it attached to his side and rarely went anywhere without it.

"Easy now," the voice said, and a moment later William relaxed as the man stepped out of the shadows. Though it had been awhile, William would have recognized that mustache anywhere.

"What are you doing here, Jack? I'm retired." William walked past the man who had convinced him to become a bounty hunter and up the few steps to his porch.

"Yeah, I heard that. Didn't really believe it though. Wild Bill Cook no longer hunting? It doesn't seem right."

"Well, it is. I've been out of the game for months. This is my life now." William motioned to the house.

"Are you really ready to settle down?"

"I settled down once before if you remember." William leaned against the side of the house and crossed his arms.

Jack's fingers traced his mustache. "That's right. You were married before. What was her name?"

"Catherine. After her death, I wasn't sure I would ever marry again, but I love Emma and I am ready." William's eyes dropped to the porch and he sighed. "Even if I weren't, this here keeps me from getting back into bounty collecting." He pointed to the scar on his neck. "Got wounded on the bounty that landed me here. Emma nursed me back to health, but I wasn't ready to settle down. Took another job, but landed in the wrong place at the wrong time and took a punch to the neck. The bullet fragments shifted, and I ended up having to have a tracheotomy. The doctors in Dallas told me I should give up the hunting life. So, I'll ask you again, Jack, what are you doing here?"

"It's Holden."

William froze at the mention of the name. John Holden, his first job as a Bounty Hunter and the job that had gotten Emma's late husband, Joseph, killed. "What about him?"

"Can we talk inside?" Jack motioned to the

front door.

William debated for a moment before nodding. He led the way through the mostly empty living room into the kitchen area where the table and chairs he had recently finished sat. He pointed to one and pulled out a second one for himself.

"So, what about Holden?"

Jack took a deep breath and ran his right hand over his mustache again and down his chin. "After we picked up Holden, he was being held in the Dallas jail until his trial. About a week ago, he managed to disarm a guard and escape."

The thought turned William's stomach over. John Holden had been notoriously evil before he was arrested and having him out again was an unsettling thought, but it was no longer William's fight. "I'm sorry to hear that, but you have great men. I'm sure you'll be able to capture him again."

"There's more, Bill."

"It's William, now."

Jack nodded and then dropped his eyes to the tabletop. His index finger tapped a few times on the wood, and William bit the inside of his lip to keep from snapping at the man to spit it out.

"You remember how connected he was?" Jack raised his eyes to meet William's once again.

"Yes, I remember."

"We got word he's gotten a few highly trained and ruthless men together and wants revenge on those who put him in prison."

William stiffened. He didn't want Holden anywhere near this town, Emma, or her family.

"The worst part is that he appears to be going after the men's families. Most of us don't have many left, but…"

"MABEL?" William hadn't spoken the name in years, but she was his only family outside of Emma.

Jack looked up. "Who?"

"My half-sister." William blinked away the old memories as they began to invade. "We haven't spoken in years. How would Holden even know about her?"

"He might not." Jack sighed and tapped the table-top. "But, William, you know how dangerous he is. Holden, at least from what I gather from witnesses, it was Holden, went after my brother. James was shot at the saloon two days ago. He didn't make it. I didn't know about your sister, but I came out here to warn you and to ask you to join me. My brother lived in Roseville, so we've dispatched the Rangers there.

They'll spread out from Roseville and update the local sheriffs. I've also rounded up as many bounty hunters as I can to track him, but I want to find him first and I want you with me. Not only are you a great shot, but your sister could be in danger."

William closed his eyes as he processed the information. Roseville wasn't far from Barefoot Glen where he had grown up. Mabel probably still lived there though he hadn't spoken with her since their mother died. However, if Holden were seeking revenge, he might go to Barefoot Glen in search of William which would put everyone in his hometown in danger, including Mabel.

Emma wouldn't want him to go though. In fact, if he were honest, he felt a small sliver of fear at the thought of going. What if he didn't make it back to Emma? Or what if he received an injury that would cost him his throat and his voice? Would Emma still want to marry a man who couldn't speak, who would be unable to tell her how beautiful she was?

But it was Mabel, and while they hadn't been close, she was still his sister. And what if Holden didn't stop there? If Hardesty found him, Holden could too and then Emma and her family would be in danger as well.

"Please, William, he was my brother."

William opened his eyes. "I need to talk with Emma."

"I understand." Jack issued a curt nod. "I'll be heading out tomorrow by noon. I can't lose him. Does that give you enough time?"

No, it didn't give him enough time. He needed another few weeks to finish the house. He wanted to marry Emma first, to start a family, but he couldn't say those things aloud. "I guess it will have to. And why don't you stay here tonight? I've only got the one bed right now, but I have plenty of blankets."

"Thank you." Jack pushed his hat back a little on his head. "That's mighty nice of you."

William nodded, pushed back his chair, and led the way to the bedrooms. The house had three. One for Emma and himself and two for the children he hoped to have one day. As he set Jack up in one room, he couldn't help wondering if his decision would keep that from ever happening.

After readying for bed, William sank to his knees and looked up. "Lord, please show me the right decision. I don't want to leave Emma, but I can't let Holden kill any more families." With his piece said, William closed his eyes and tried to quiet his spirit so he could hear God's answer.

Continue reading The Scarlet Wedding

30

A FREE STORY FOR YOU

Enjoyed Lawfully Justified? Not ready to quit reading yet? If you sign up for my newsletter, you will receive Once Upon a Star, the love story of Blake and Audrey, two of my Star Lake characters, right away as my thank you gift for choosing to hang out with me.

Once Upon a Star

A high school crush....

Blake was a nerd in high school. Never noticed. Looked over. So, it was no wonder that Audrey paid no attention to him, but now that she's back in town...

Audrey left Star Lake to pursue acting, but when she ends up pregnant and alone, she finds herself forced to return home.

Can Blake show Audrey a new side? Will she trust him enough to stay?

Read on for a taste of Once Upon a Star....

31

ONCE UPON A STAR PREVIEW

A udrey tried to peek around the nurses leaning over the silver table, obscuring the view of the thing she wanted to see most.

"Are you ready, Mom?" The head nurse, a kind, older woman with just a touch of gray in her dark hair, turned to Audrey, a tiny blue package in her arms.

Mom. The word had never applied to her, and she wasn't sure it fit. Was she ready? Probably not. Would she ever be completely ready? Probably not. But that didn't change reality. She tucked a strand of blond hair behind her ear and nodded.

"Here's your son." The nurse held the swaddled bundle out to her. Audrey opened her hands, unsure of what the nurse wanted her to do. The nurse's face softened and her warm brown eyes sparkled. With one hand, she adjusted Audrey's arms to place the tiny bundle in them. "Hold him like this." She demonstrated the proper technique. "You always want to support his head."

Audrey nodded, trying to keep her arms from shaking. She was afraid to breathe, afraid to move, but mostly afraid she'd drop the infant, so she kept her eyes glued to him. Would he shatter like a piece of glass? The image sent a shiver down her spine. She didn't want to find out.

The nurse's eyes twinkled as she watched Audrey adjust and readjust her holding position. "There is a bassinet here." She pointed at a clear plastic tub that looked like a large shoe box on top of a wheeled table. It didn't look comfortable to Audrey, and she wondered how a baby slept in it. "If you want to take him walking, you need to put him in the bassinet, okay?"

"Do I hold him the rest of the time?" As much as she was enjoying the baby in her arms, what happened when she needed to sleep or use the bathroom?

The woman chuckled. "You hold him as much as you want and put him down when you need a break. We'll come in every few hours to check on you, and we'll show you how to change his diaper and dress him. You'll be a pro before you know it. Don't worry." She patted Audrey's arm like her grandmother used to when she asked a silly question, and then the nurse walked out of the room, still smiling and shaking her head.

Audrey's eyes dropped to the sleeping baby. His shock of dark hair reminded her of his father, the olive-skinned Italian who had charmed her with his fast tongue. She hoped it was the only trait Cayden would get from him. The world didn't need another heartbreaker. "I have no idea what we'll do, Cayden, but we'll figure something out."

BLAKE TURNED the glass on the countertop and glanced up at Max who leaned against the back counter, arms folded across his chest as if he were waiting for the answer to a question. The green of his plaid shirt matched the faded ball cap turned backwards on his head. "Sorry, did you say something? I'm distracted; it's just getting close to Christmas, and I miss Connie." A vision of the day she left popped into his head.

Blake opened the door, expecting to see Connie on the other side in her Sunday best. The church service started in half an hour. Though Connie stood there, his smile faded as he took in her jeans and t-shirt. There was no requirement of the patrons to dress up, but Connie always wore a dress or skirt. "What's going on?" Blake asked.

Connie bit her lip and her eyes fell to the ground. "I wanted to say goodbye."

"Goodbye?"

"I can't stay any longer, Blake." Her eyes lifted to meet his, and he saw the shimmer of liquid in them. "I hoped I could make a life here, but I'm a city girl. I miss the lights and night life. I miss the excitement."

"But, we were discussing marriage last week." Blake struggled to make her words compute in his brain.

"I know," she nodded, "and that's what got me thinking. The thought of living the rest of my life here is depressing, so though I love you, I have to say goodbye." She leaned in and pecked his cheek before flashing a sad smile and walking back to her car.

With a heavy heart, Blake watched her drive away before shutting the door and leaning against it. His brain tried to make sense of her departure.

"I get it," Max said, leaning forward and dispersing Blake's memory. "It's not the same, but you're welcome to spend Christmas with Layla and me.

Blake offered a half smile. "I'll consider it, but it's your first Christmas together. You've been in love with that woman since I've known you and I don't want to be a third wheel. Besides, I'll probably hit the Christmas Eve service at church and spend the day with my mom. She's been lonely without my father around."

Max shrugged and turned back to the kitchen to finish serving the lunch crowd.

Blake took a bite of his hamburger, but while he knew it was delicious—Max was known for his burgers—it held no taste in his current mood. He fished a few dollars out of his wallet, laid the money on the counter, picked up his coat, and walked out the door.

The McAllister development where he worked sat a mile up the road, but as he still had fifteen minutes remaining on his lunch break, he decided to walk through downtown. His own house resided on the quiet outskirts of town, so other than hanging out with Max at The Diner, he didn't spend much time in the downtown area.

Blake pulled his coat tighter as the winter air bit through the heavy wool. Star Lake generally received one or two good snowfalls every winter, and though Christmas was still a few weeks away, the chill in the air made him believe the first snow was coming.

He didn't mind the snow, but he enjoyed it more when he had someone to share the experience with. Curling in front of the fireplace alone held little appeal.

AUDREY SHOVED the last item in her suitcase and pushed down on the bulging bag as she tugged on the zipper.

"Where are you going to go?" Desiree asked, leaning against the doorframe.

Desiree was Audrey's roommate, and the two were about as different as night and day. Where Audrey was pale and blond, Desiree had darker skin and long dark hair.

"The only place I can," Audrey said with a sigh. "Home."

The thought held little appeal. Her wealthy parents had given her access to her trust fund at eighteen, and Audrey had opted to move to LA to try her hand at acting. At first, it had been fun. She'd found a few jobs and been in a few commercials, but then the jobs had become fewer and farther between, and after she ended up pregnant, they had dried up completely. Now all the money she had saved was almost gone.

Desiree's nose scrunched in disgust. "You'd go back to that tiny town, why?"

"I haven't had a job in months Dez, my savings have run out, and I can't go to work without someone to watch Cayden. If I go home, I can get help from my parents until I get back on my feet."

At least she hoped they would help. They hadn't been too happy when she decided not to go to college, but she didn't think they would turn their grandson away, even if they didn't want to help her.

Desiree shrugged and flicked her hair behind her bony shoulder. "Nothing in the world would make me return to my crappy hometown."

Audrey knew Desiree's home life had been rough, but while she hadn't wanted to grow up under her mother's thumb, it hadn't been a bad childhood. "I don't know if I'll ever be back, but I wish you luck."

After a quick hug, Audrey picked up Cayden's car seat, slung her bag over her shoulder, and left the apartment she had called home for the last few years.

Click here to sign up for my newsletter and continue reading Once Upon a Star.

WOULD YOU LEAVE A REVIEW?

As an author, I highly appreciate the feedback I get from my readers. It helps others make an informed decision before buying my book. If you enjoyed this book, please review at your retailer.

If you would like to keep up on Sage Creek, join my newsletter.

Do you like free books? I'm offering a free sample of my next book Free Sample!

THE STORY DOESN'T END!

You've met a few people and fallen in love….

I bet you're wondering how you can meet everyone else.

Star Lake Series:

When Love Returns: The first in the Star Lake series. Presley Hays and Brandon Scott were best friends in High School until Morgan entered their town and stole Brandon's heart. Devastated, Presley takes a scholarship to Le Cordon Bleu, but five years later, she is back in Star Lake after a tough breakup. Brandon thought he'd never return to Star Lake after Morgan left him and his daughter Joy, but when his father needs help, he returns home and finds more than he bargained for. Can Presley and Brandon forget past hurts or will their stubborn natures keep them apart forever?

Once Upon a Star: The second book in the Star Lake series. Audrey left Star Lake to pursue acting, but after an unplanned pregnancy her jobs and her money dwindled, leaving her no option except to return home and start over. Blake was the quintessential nerd in high school and was never able to tell Audrey how he felt. Now that he's gained confidence and some muscle, will he finally be able to reveal his feelings? Once Upon a Star will take you back to Christmas in Star Lake. Revisit your favorite characters and meet a few ones in this sweet Christmas read.

Love Conquers All: Lanie Perkins Hall never imagined being divorced at thirty. Nor did she imagine falling for an old friend, but when she runs into Azarius Jacobson, she can't deny the attraction. As they begin to spend more time together, Lanie struggles with the fact Azarius keeps his past a secret. What is he hiding? And will she ever be able to get him to open up? Azarius Jacobson has loved Lanie Perkins Hall from the moment he saw her, but issues from his past have left him guarded. Now that he has another chance with her, will he find the courage to share his life with her? Or will his emotional walls create a barrier that will leave him alone once more? Find out in this heartfelt, emotional third book (stand alone) in the Star Lake series.

The Heartbeats Series:

Where It All Began: Sandra Baker thought her life was on the right track until she ended up pregnant. Her boyfriend, not wanting the baby, pushes her to have an abortion. After the procedure, Sandra's life falls apart, and she turns to alcohol. Her relationship ends, and she struggles to find meaning in her life. When she meets Henry Dobbs, a strong Christian man, she begins to wonder if God would accept her. Will she tell Henry her darkest secret? And will she ever be able to forgive herself and find healing? Find out in this emotional love story.

The Power of Prayer: Callie Green thought she had her whole life planned out until her fiance left her at the altar. When her carefully laid plans crumble, she begins to make mistakes at work and engage in uncharacteristic activities. After a mistake nearly costs her her job, she cashes in her honeymoon tickets for some time away. There she meets JD, a charming Christian man who, even though she is not a believer, captures her interest. Before their relationship can deepen, Callie's ex-fiance shows back up in her life and she is forced to choose between Daniel and JD. Who will she choose and how will her choice affect the rest of her life? Find out in this touching novel.

When Hearts Collide: Amanda Adams has always been a Christian, but she's a novice at relationships. When she meets Caleb, her emotions get the best of her and she ignores the sign that something is amiss. Will she find out before it's too late? Jared Masterson is still healing from his girlfriend's strange rejection and disappearance when he meets Amanda. She captivates his heart, but can he save her from making the biggest mistake of her life? A must read for mothers and daughters. Though part of the series and the first of the college spin off series, it is a stand alone book and can be read separately.

A Past Forgiven: Jess Peterson has lived a life of abuse and lost her self worth, but when she is paired with a Christian roommate, she begins to wonder if there is a loving father looking down on her. Her decisions lead her one way, but when she ends up pregnant, she must make some major changes. Chad Michelson is healing from his own past and uses meaningless relationships to hide his pain, but when Jess becomes pregnant, he begins to wonder about the meaning of life. Can he step up and be there for Jess and the baby?

Sweet Billionaires Series:

The Billionaire's Secret: Maxwell Banks was the ultimate player until he found himself caring for a daughter he didn't know he had. Can he change to become the role model she needs? Alyssa Miller hasn't had the best luck with past relationships, so why is she falling for the one man who is sure to break her heart? Though nearly complete opposites, feelings develop, but can Max really change his philandering ways? Or will one mistake seal his fate forever?

A Brush with a Billionaire: Brent just wanted to finish his novel in peace, but when his car breaks down in Sweet Grove, he is forced to deal with a female mechanic and try to get along. Sam thought she had given up on city boys, but when Brent shows up in her shop, she finds herself fighting attraction. Will their stubborn natures keep them apart or can a small town festival bring them together?

The Billionaire's Christmas Miracle: Drew Devonshire is captivated by the woman he meets at a masquerade ball, but who is she? Gwen Rodgers is a teacher, but when she pretends to be her friend and meets Drew at a masquerade ball, her world gets thrown upside down.

The Billionaire's Cowboy Groom: Carrie Bliss finally found the man she wants to marry but there's just one little problem. She's technically still married. Cal Roper hasn't seen her in years but his heart still belongs to his wife. When she returns to town requesting a divorce, can he convince her they belong together?

The Lawkeeper Series:

Lawfully Matched: Kate Whidby doesn't want to impose on her newly married brother after their parents die, so she accepts a mail order bride offer in the paper. Little does she know the man she intends to marry has a dark past, sending her fleeing into a neighboring town and into Jesse Jenning's life. Jesse never wanted to be in law enforcement, but after a band of robbers kills his fiancee, he dons the badge and swears revenge. Will he find his fiancee's killer? And when Kate flies into his life, will he be able to put his painful past behind him in order to love again?

Lawfully Justified: William Cook turns to bounty hunting after losing his wife. When he suffers a life-threatening injury, he is forced to stay in town with an intriguing woman. Emma Stewart has moved back in with her widowed father, the town doctor, but she still longs for a family of her own, so no one is more surprised than she is when she starts to develop feeling for the bounty hunter, who hides his heart of gold behind a rugged exterior. Can Emma offer William a reason to stay? Can William find a way to heal from his broken past to start a future with Emma? Or will a haunting secret take away all the possibilities of this budding romance?

The Scarlet Wedding: William and Emma are planning their wedding, but an outbreak and a return from his past force them to change their plans. Is a happily ever after still in their future?

Lawfully Redeemed: Dani Higgins is a K9 cop looking to make a name for herself, but she finds herself at the mercy of a stranger after an accident. Calvin Phillips just wanted to help his brother, but somehow he ended up in the middle of a police investigation and caring for the woman trying to bring his brother in.

Lawfully Pursued: SWAT Officer Jesse Calhoun wasn't looking for love, much less with a billionaire's daughter, but Brie is hard to ignore. Brie Carter was just looking for a little fun but when a bet goes wrong, how does she keep from losing the man she's fallen in love with?

The Still Small Voice Series:

The Still Small Voice: Jordan Wright was searching for something after she gave her son up for adoption. What she found was God, and she began receiving visions. But can she trust Him when he asks her to do something big? Kat Jameson had long been a lukewarm Christian, but when her friend dies and she begins seeing lights, she thinks she is going crazy. Then she meets someone with a message for her. Will she be able to give up control and do what is asked of her?

A Spark in the Darkness coming soon!

Blushing Brides Series:

The Cowboy's Reality Bride: Tyler Hall just wanted to find love, but the women he dated wanted more than his small-town life provided. He gets more than he bargained for when he ends up on a reality dating show and falls for a woman who is not a contestant. Laney Swann has been running from her past for years, but it takes meeting a man on a reality dating show to make her see there's no need to run.

The Reality Bride's Baby: Laney wants

nothing more than a baby, but when she starts feeling dizzy is it pregnancy or something more serious?

The Producer's Unlikely Bride: Justin Miller had given up on love, but when his image needs help, he finds himself needing the aid of a stranger who just happens to be a romance writer. Ava McDermott is waiting for the perfect love, but after agreeing to a fake relationship with Justin, she finds herself falling for real.

The Soldier's Steadfast Bride: coming soon

The Cop's Fiery Bride: coming soon

Stand Alones:

Love Renewed: This books is part of the multi author second chance series. When fate reunites high school sweethearts separated by life's choices, can they find a second chance at love at a snowy lodge amid a little mystery?

Her children's early reader chapter book series:

The Wishing Stone #1: Dangerous Dinosaur

The Wishing Stone #2: Dragon Dilemma

The Wishing Stone #3: Mesmerizing Mermaids

The Wishing Stone #4: Pyramid Puzzle

The Wishing Stone Inspirations 1: Mary's Miracle

authorloranahoopes.com

loranahoopes@gmail.com

To see a list of all her books

authorloranahoopes.com

loranahoopes@gmail.com

ABOUT THE AUTHOR

Lorana Hoopes is an inspirational author originally from Texas but now living in the PNW with her husband and three children. When not writing, she can be seen kickboxing at the gym, singing, or acting on stage. One day, she hopes to retire from teaching and write full time.

www.ingramcontent.com/pod-product-compliance
Lightning Source LLC
Chambersburg PA
CBHW020637180626
46816CB00003B/1003